"Anyone for the hot tub? Aren't you coming, Mollie?" Alex flashed his lazy grin, and Mollie wavered, not sure she wanted to compete with the voluptuous Sachi in a borrowed bathing suit. If only she had her new mauve bikini!

"I didn't bring my bathing suit," she explained.

"You're such a riot," Alex grinned. "Who needs a bathing suit? Come on, the spa's out back."

Mollie, gulping hard, wasn't sure that she'd understood. "Are you serious?"

Alex's bland expression convinced her more quickly than any protest.

"I mean, uh, in a minute. I need—where's the powder room?"

"Oh." Alex nodded. "Just off the front hall. Come on back when you're ready."

"Sure," Mollie agreed, and scurried off to find the bathroom.

Safely inside, Mollie stared into a large gilt framed mirror at her own reflection. Nude?

FAWCETT GIRLS ONLY BOOKS

Sisters

THREE'S A CROWD #1

TOO LATE FOR LOVE #2

THE KISS #3

SECRETS AT SEVENTEEN #4

ALWAYS A PAIR #5

ON THIN ICE #6

STAR QUALITY #7

MAKING WAVES #8

TOO MANY COOKS #9

SISTERS

TOO MANY COOKS

Jennifer Cole

FAWCETT GIRLS ONLY • NEW YORK

RLI: $\dfrac{\text{VL: Grades 5 + up}}{\text{IL: Grades 6 + up}}$

A Fawcett Girls Only Book
Published by Ballantine Books
Copyright © 1987 by Cloverdale Press, Inc.

Library of Congress Catalog Card Number: 86-91372

ISBN 0-449-13209-9

Manufactured in the United States of America

First Edition: March 1987

Chapter 1

"*She'll be all right, won't she, Dad?*" Fourteen-year-old Mollie Lewis, her blue eyes almost overflowing with tears, sniffed loudly as she twisted her handkerchief into another damp knot.

"Mollie, would you stop bugging Dad!" Cindy Lewis, just turned sixteen and feeling the mantle of adulthood about to descend upon her tanned shoulders, stopped pacing in the hospital waiting room and turned to face her younger sister. "Don't be such a worrywart. Mom's going to be fine; the doctor *promised*."

Nicole Lewis, at seventeen the oldest of the three Lewis sisters, forced herself to smile. Like Cindy, she, too, struggled to maintain an optimistic facade. She sat quietly on the waiting room bench, a magazine forgotten in her lap; only her tenseness revealed her inner anxiety. "It's only an appendectomy, Mollie."

Mollie's eyes widened. "But it was an emergency!"

"Nicole means that this is fairly minor surgery, Mollie," Richard Lewis told his youngest daughter, reaching out to ruffle her blond curls. "Your mother shouldn't have any problems." Lines of tension etched around his good-natured blue eyes belied his reassuring words.

Mollie sniffed again. Who could have guessed that the lighthearted family barbecue that began Sunday afternoon would end up with their mother in the hospital Emergency Room?

It had been a marvelous spring day; balmy temperatures and blue skies with only an occasional wispy cloud. Excited about the beginning of the spring break, all the girls were in a cheerful mood, relishing the thought of their extralong vacation. They had an extra week off this year to allow renovations of their high school to be completed. Two full weeks with no school.

"I can hear those waves calling me now," Cindy had joked. A dedicated surfer, she had talked nonstop about the beach parties she and her friends had planned. She couldn't wait to meet Duffy and Anna and Grant at the beach first thing in the morning. Grant was the first boy with whom Cindy had ever been more than just friends. They had been dating, with only minor squabbles, since the beginning of the school year.

"Heather and I leave on our Catalina cruise Friday," Mollie had reminded her family. "A whole weekend on Catalina Island. I can't wait, and I saw the greatest bikini at the mall yesterday. Now all I need is a small advance on my allowance so I'll have it in time for the trip." She had looked hopefully toward her father, and her face had fallen when she saw him laughing as he turned the ribs on the barbecue.

"Mollie, you're in debt up to your ears right now," he had said.

"In your case, that's not too bad, shrimp," Cindy had quipped.

Mollie had drawn her petite frame up as tall as possible and stuck out her tongue at her sister, then continued to set the patio table. "Well, since Nicole's making so much money with her part-time modeling, maybe she could lend me—"

"I need all my extra money for my week in New England," Nicole had told her little sister, ignoring Mollie's wistful glance. "And I deliberately didn't schedule any modeling assignments over spring break. After I get back, I want a little free time to myself."

"Why go to New England in the spring, anyhow?" Mollie had grumbled.

"She's going to look at colleges, dummy," Cindy had said, tossing the salad with such gusto that a lettuce leaf flew out of the bowl and off the table. Winston, the Lewises' big Newfoundland, had come over to sniff at the morsel, quickly lost interest, and flopped back down on the cool brick patio. "While you go looking for boys!"

"So?" Mollie had glared at Cindy, but Nicole, uncovering a steaming pot of baked beans, had cut the incipient quarrel short.

"Dad's taking off the ribs. We're ready to eat," she had said, and the other two girls had hurried to sit down and join their parents in the delicious meal.

No one had noticed, at first, that Laura Lewis was unusually quiet. When the meal ended, she had asked the girls to clean up. Cindy and Mollie had already picked up a pile of plates and bowls and started for the kitchen, when Nicole asked, "Mother, *qu'est-ce qu'il y a?* Are you all right?"

And Richard Lewis, noticing how pale his wife's face had become, had pushed Winston out of his way and hurried to her side. "What's wrong, Laura?"

"Just a little stomachache," their mother had told them, trying to smile. "Probably overdid it on your dad's delicious ribs. I'll just lie down a while, and I'm sure I'll be fine."

Mrs. Lewis had gone upstairs, but resting didn't alleviate her discomfort. Instead, her abdominal pains had become rapidly worse, finally resulting in a trip to the hospital Emergency Room in the early hours of Monday morning.

A blood test and exam had confirmed the doctor's suspicion, and Mrs. Lewis had been prepared for surgery. Although Richard Lewis had left his daughters at home when he drove his wife to the hospital, after a phone call to let them know what was happening, the three girls had piled into the station wagon, an anxious Nicole at the wheel, to join their dad in the waiting room while their mother went into surgery.

That seemed like days ago, Mollie thought now, glancing out the window. Behind the half-drawn blinds, she saw the early morning sun lighting the hospital lawns. She sighed. No matter how many times everyone assured her that this was not a major emergency, her instincts insisted that something could go wrong unexpectedly. That awful thought, plus the antiseptic smell of the hospital corridors, had tied her stomach into as many knots as the handkerchief she twisted nervously in her hands.

"What's taking so long?" Cindy unconsciously echoed her sister's thoughts as she paced up and down the beige carpet. She had even tossed aside her Walkman, too impatient to listen to her usual rock music.

Richard Lewis looked at his watch for the hundredth time. "Doctor Martin said he would tell us as soon as they were out of surgery. It shouldn't be much longer."

"You said that half an hour ago," Cindy complained.

"*Mon dieu,* you're going to wear a path in the

carpet," Nicole pointed out, her usually serene tone sharp.

"Who gives a hoot?" Cindy retorted, whirling on her sister. She considered telling Nicole just what a pain her incessant French phrases really were. Nerves raw from worry over their mother, neither girl needed any provocation to begin a quarrel. But their dispute ended as suddenly as it had begun.

"Mr. Lewis?" The doctor, still clad in surgical green, had been unnoticed by any of the Lewises, but now they all turned quickly toward the doorway.

"How is she?" Richard Lewis asked eagerly.

The doctor smiled and even Mollie relaxed.

"The operation went smoothly," the surgeon answered. "She's in the recovery room; you can take a quick peek if you like, then no visitors for a few hours. She'll sleep most of the day."

Richard Lewis, needing no further prompting, disappeared down the hallway, and the three girls grinned at each other.

Cindy hugged Mollie, who didn't object. "I told you she'd be fine!" Cindy said, already forgetting her fears.

"This is great!" Nicole said. "We'd better get home and straighten the house. I don't want mother to see what a mess we left this morning."

The doctor's smile widened. "You don't have to rush. Your mother won't be coming home for several days."

"What about her work?" Nicole said with a worried frown. The other two girls looked at each other.

"What does she do?" the doctor asked.

"She runs her own catering business, Movable Feasts," Nicole told him, "from a shop in town. This is one of her busiest times of the year, with spring weddings and all."

The surgeon shook his head. "I don't want her to set foot in her shop for at least two weeks. Even after that, no heavy lifting or overly strenuous activity for some time."

Nicole looked worried, but she remembered to thank the doctor before he departed.

"Let's go home," Cindy suggested. "I'm starving. How about a big breakfast to celebrate, Nicole?"

"Mais oui," Nicole agreed, but even Cindy could tell her heart wasn't in it. "But what's Mom going to do about the shop?"

"Carol's there," Mollie reminded them, and Nicole nodded at the mention of their mother's capable assistant.

"Carol can't do everything alone, and the part-time girl just quit. We've got to help out. Thank goodness for spring break!"

"What about your trip to New England?" Cindy demanded.

"C'est la vie. That can wait. We don't want Mother worried about the business. She might try to go back to work before she's ready."

"You're right," Cindy agreed, with a private sigh for all the glorious surfing she was about to forgo. "We can have fun any time; Mom's peace of mind is more important."

"Don't forget about me." Mollie, not about to be outdone spoke up quickly. "I can work, too!"

"What about your plans to go to Catalina with Heather?" Nicole raised her brows.

"If you can give up a trip to the East Coast to inspect colleges, I can forget a weekend cruise," Mollie said, beaming over her own benevolence.

Cindy looked down her nose at her little sister. "You'll probably be more of a handicap than a help," she said bluntly.

"I will not!"

"Hush," Nicole warned. "Here's Dad."

They all turned eagerly. "Did you see her?" Cindy demanded.

"Is she really okay?" Mollie asked worriedly.

"Is she still asleep?" Nicole put in.

Their father, his expression much more relaxed than just a few minutes earlier, reported, "She opened her eyes when I kissed her and said, 'Don't add too much vanilla!' Then she went back to sleep. She looks wonderful."

All the girls grinned, happy to have this family crisis behind them.

"We're going to help out at the shop," Nicole told him, "so Mother won't rush back to work."

"What about your plans for spring break?" Mr. Lewis asked, raising his brows.

"Who cares about that when Mom needs help?"

"You know she'll worry about the shop, and the doctor said—"

"All right, all right." Their father threw up his hands and smiled at them proudly. "I think this is a very fine gesture for you to make, girls. Your mother will be pleased. But we'd better get home now; we'll come back this evening when she's more alert. And there's one thing we don't want to put off, even for this."

"What?" Cindy looked ready to argue, but her belligerent expression turned to excitement at her dad's answer.

"You have an appointment this afternoon at the Department of Motor Vehicles, remember?"

"Oh, my gosh," Cindy yelped. "My driver's test!"

Chapter 2

*T*he girls drove home in the family station wagon, followed by their father in the sedan. As Nicole carefully turned out of the hospital drive, Mollie, in the backseat, said, "Just think, after today, Cindy will have her license. I'll be the only Lewis who can't drive! I hate being the youngest!"

Familiar with Mollie's theatrics, neither sister offered any sympathy.

"*If* she passes her test," Nicole pointed out.

Cindy threw her a baleful glance. "Of course I'll pass! I've been practicing for six months, and I took Driver's Ed at school."

"*C'est vrai,*" Nicole agreed, grinning slightly. "Mother and Dad will be thrilled to be free of your pestering."

"Well, I couldn't drive alone with a learner's

permit; you know that." Cindy, feeling unfairly criticized, looked stormy.

Nicole, catching a glimpse of her sister's expression, quickly changed her tone. Their dad wouldn't be happy to come home to a family quarrel, not after all the worry about their mother.

"I'm just teasing, hothead," she told the middle Lewis. "I'm sure you'll pass the test. And it *is* very exciting to get your license; I remember how thrilled I was."

Cindy, whose flares of temper usually subsided as quickly as they came, grinned. "Just wait till you see *me* driving home this afternoon."

As soon as they reached their sprawling, red-roofed, Spanish-style home, the girls all hurried off in different directions. Nicole stopped to feed Winston and the two cats, who had been forgotten in the early morning exodus to the hospital, then, humming beneath her breath, began to whip eggs and cream for french toast.

Cindy headed for her room to review her much-thumbed driver's manual, although she was fairly sure she had the whole book memorized by now. And Mollie headed for the phone to recount, with great dramatic emphasis, their mother's trip to the hospital. Suitably embellished, the story would undoubtedly impress all of her friends.

After a delicious brunch of french toast and lightly browned sausages, with fresh fruit on the side, Nicole, who had not slept well the night before—she had been the only one of the three who woke when her parents left for the Emergency Room—decided to indulge herself with a nap before straightening the house.

Mollie made a beeline back to the telephone, and Cindy headed upstairs to take a shower and dress for her big test.

She was waiting impatiently when her dad returned from his office.

"Ready to go, Skipper?"

"I've been ready for almost an hour," Cindy assured him, trying not to sound accusing.

"Sorry, I had a couple of plans to glance over. But we'll be at the DMV office in plenty of time. The new appointment system should cut down on the long lines, at least."

They were headed out the door when Mollie put her head around the corner of the hall.

"Can I come watch?"

"Sure." Richard Lewis nodded.

"Dad!" Cindy protested. "I don't need a cheering section; I don't want my kid sister tagging along."

Mollie's smile crumbled. "I won't get in your way. I just want to see what you have to do, Cindy. *Someday* my chance is going to come, you know."

"I don't see that it will hurt, Cindy," their dad said in a mild tone. "No passengers are allowed to go on the test drive, so you don't have to worry about Mollie sitting in the backseat."

"Okay, I guess," Cindy agreed reluctantly.

True to Mr. Lewis's prediction, they arrived at the Department of Motor Vehicles and found only a couple of people ahead of Cindy at the designated counter.

Cindy took her place in line, while Mr. Lewis and Mollie retreated to a row of seats at the side of the big room. Clutching her learner's permit, her certificate from the high school Driver's Ed program, and her birth certificate, Cindy mumbled to herself as she waited. "Red curb—no parking at any time; white curb—passenger pickup only. No. Wait a minute. Is that a green curb? Oh no!"

Suddenly all the facts she had studied so carefully got jumbled up inside her head like pieces of a jigsaw puzzle. She took a deep breath as her turn came to step up to the counter.

"Do you have an appointment?"

"Yes," Cindy told the grayhaired lady.

"Name?"

"Cindy Lewis."

Cindy handed over all her documents, and the woman behind the counter pulled out several forms, then handed the stack of paper back to the nervous teenager. "Here is the written exam; you go to that section of the room. When you finish, take the exam to counter F."

Cindy nodded and hurried over to the examining section. A large sign warned her not to discuss the questions with anyone and proclaimed the penalties for cheating. Cindy, who had never cheated on a test in her life, ignored the posted warning and concentrated on the long slip of paper.

To her relief, once she started reading the questions, all the jumbled information inside her head began to sort itself out. Cindy marked her answers quickly. Only two questions stumped her, even after she read them several times. She could not remember how many feet from the curb one could legally park, or what the penalty was for driving under the influence of alcohol. She finally made a couple of guesses, then turned in her test.

"Only one incorrect. Very good." She smiled at Cindy, who grinned back. One hurdle down!

"Now go back outside, pull your car into the lane marked for the road test, and wait your turn. Give the examiner this form. Good luck."

"Thanks," Cindy said, then headed back to find her dad.

"I passed the first test, Dad. Now for the hard part. I need the keys, please."

Mr. Lewis handed over the car keys, and Cindy, swallowing hard to calm the butterflies in her stomach, walked back to the parking lot to collect the Lewis station wagon.

"How's it going, Cindy?" a familiar voice asked.

Cindy whirled around, squinting against the bright sunlight, and gaped at the tall red-haired boy beside her.

"Duffy! What are you doing here?"

"Came to wish you good luck, of course." The

tall boy, dressed in his usual T-shirt and cutoffs, his old blue knapsack swung over his shoulder, grinned at her. "From the old, experienced driver to the novice."

Cindy, knowing perfectly well that Duffy had passed his own driver's test hardly a month before, snorted. "How did you know when I'd be here?"

"Are you kidding? It's all you've talked about for the last two weeks."

"Oh," Cindy looked a little sheepish. "I guess I've been a pain, huh?"

"You got it," Duffy agreed cheerfully. "Don't you dare fail the test; nobody at school wants to hear you moan for *another* two weeks."

"I won't," Cindy assured him, managing not to cross her fingers as she spoke. "I've already passed the written exam; now comes the road test."

"Oh," For some reason, Duffy's grin widened. "That should be interesting."

"Piece of cake," Cindy boasted. "Well, I've got to get in line. See you later."

"Sure."

Cindy promptly forgot her surfing buddy as she pulled the car around into the line marked ROAD TEST ONLY.

She waited impatiently for the drivers in the two cars ahead of her to finish their tests, drumming her fingers on the steering wheel as she whistled to herself. Her own driver's license! Life was sweet.

"Have you taken your test yet?"

Cindy glanced up as the last vehicle in front of her pulled away and saw Mollie peering into the car.

"Get lost, shrimp!"

"I just wondered how it was going." Mollie sounded hurt, and she drew back quickly. "Pardon me for living."

To Cindy's relief, she saw her little sister head back inside the building. It wasn't that Mollie *meant* to be a walking disaster, but strange things sometimes happened in the vicinity of the youngest Lewis. This was no time for mishaps!

Cindy, who was now first in line, sat up straighter when she saw the examiner walking toward her car. She could feel her adrenaline pumping despite her best efforts to be calm. This was really it!

The examiner, a stern-faced lady with short hair, seemed to be a woman of few words.

"Paper?" she demanded, and Cindy quickly handed over the form.

"Turn on your signals please, right and left," the woman said as she walked to the front of the car to watch. "Now the lights. Dim them."

Cindy followed instructions while the woman made notations on her form. Then she walked to the back of the Lewis car, and Cindy, watching anxiously in the rearview mirror, saw the woman jerk her head in apparent surprise. What was wrong?

The woman stalked back to the side of the car, her expression offended. "You cannot take the road test in a car without proper plates!"

"What?" Aghast, Cindy jumped out and hurried around to the back of the car. To her horror, she saw that the California license plate had been removed, replaced by a comic plate that proclaimed in large letters, TEEN SURFER—I LIVE FOR THE BEACH!

"Mollie!" Cindy muttered through clenched teeth. "How could she do this to me? I'll kill her!"

To the grim-faced examiner, Cindy pleaded, "It's a joke—my little sister did it. Please, just give me five minutes, and I'll get my license plate back."

The woman, who didn't appear remotely amused, snapped, "Five minutes and no more!"

Cindy ran for the building, rage threatening to overwhelm her. Fortunately, she spotted Mollie talking to an unfamiliar blond-headed boy as soon as she entered the big building.

"Oh, hi, Cindy. Finished already? Did you pass? This is—" Mollie began, when Cindy, irritated past all restraint, took her sister by the shoulders and began to shake her small frame.

"Cin—Cindy!" Mollie yelped, while the boy she had been talking to eased away from this ferocious newcomer.

"Where is it?" Cindy demanded. "Give it back, right now, or I'll fail the test and have to wait a week before I can schedule another appointment!"

"What are you talking about?" Mollie wailed, trying to escape her frantic sister. "Let go of me!"

Cindy paused, releasing her sister, whose curly blond hair had fallen across her face. Mollie looked genuinely bewildered.

"Didn't you switch plates on me?" Cindy asked.

"Why would I do that?" Mollie asked, offended. "You always blame things on me."

"Then who—" Cindy wrinkled her nose, then slapped her forehead as enlightenment came. "Duffy! That rat. He's making me suffer for all the time he spent listening to me worry about the test. Wait till I find him!"

"Oh, that reminds me," Mollie said as Cindy began to look wildly around the room. "He said to give you this." She took a large manila envelope from her oversized handbag. Cindy grabbed it.

Sure enough, there was the purloined plate, along with a scrawled note that said, "Ha, ha."

"Just you wait, Duffy Duncan," Cindy murmured, then ran for her car.

While the bleak-faced examiner waited, pointedly looking at her watch, Cindy quickly replaced the license plate and took her place behind the steering wheel. As soon as the examiner seated herself on the passenger side, the road test began.

"Turn right at the street entrance," the woman said.

Cindy, her already-frayed nerves almost breaking after her near disaster, stepped on the gas too abruptly, and the car started with a lurch. The examiner shook her head and made a note on her clipboard. Cindy bit back a groan and concentrated on her driving.

Although she drove very carefully, she felt perspiration gather on her forehead as the road test continued. The unsmiling examiner, occasionally making notations on her sheet, gave curt directions and never once commented on Cindy's performance. By the time they drove back into the DMV parking lot, Cindy was convinced she had failed the test, and she—who never cried—had to bite her lip to keep it from trembling. She waited while the woman finished writing, then accepted the paper silently, afraid to ask the results.

"Take this to counter F."

"What for?" Cindy managed to ask, sure that she'd blown her big day.

"For the eye test and photo," the woman said, as if it were understood.

"You mean I passed?" Cindy, her spirits recovering rapidly, sat up straighter.

The woman nodded curtly, then opened the door and departed to find her next victim.

"Oh, my gosh." Cindy sighed in relief. "I don't believe it."

She finished the rest of the required paperwork, passed her eye test, smiled for the camera, and then, blissfully happy, accepted her temporary license.

She floated back to the waiting area where Mr.

Lewis and Mollie waited. "I made it!" Cindy cried, and her father patted her on the back.

"I knew you could do it. Good job, Cindy."

Mollie, who didn't say a word, looked like she was sulking.

Cindy, suddenly guilt-stricken over her mistaken assumption, turned to her sister. "I'm sorry, shrimp. I thought you were the one playing tricks."

"You always blame me." Mollie sounded truly bereft.

"I am sorry, Mollie."

"You ruined my chances with Pete!"

"Who?" Both Cindy and her father stared at the smallest Lewis.

"This neat guy that I met waiting in one of the lines—you scared him away." Mollie sounded so crestfallen that the other two smiled.

"Easy come, easy go," Cindy pointed out heartlessly. "Let's go home."

Back at the Lewis residence, Cindy, who had proudly driven home, with her father beside her and Mollie still sulking in the backseat, was the first inside the house.

"I passed, Nicole," she yelled.

"I'm right here," her older sister answered from the pantry. "You don't have to shout."

"Oh, sorry. Anyhow, I did it. I got my license."

"*Très bien,* Cindy. Congratulations."

"California drivers, look out," Mollie said from behind them.

"What's with her?" Nicole asked, surprised at Mollie's sulky tone.

"Let's eat a quick dinner, girls, and go visit your mother," Richard Lewis said, coming into the kitchen behind them.

"I've already made egg salad sandwiches on croissants and a spinach salad," Nicole said.

"Great." Mr. Lewis smiled at his eldest daughter. "I'll just wash up and then we can eat."

He left the kitchen, followed by Mollie, still frowning.

"What's her problem?"

"She thinks I killed a budding romance. I'll explain later." Cindy headed for the table. "This looks good, Nicole. I'm starved."

But her sister didn't seem to hear. She was pouring glasses of lemonade, a look of concern on her face.

"Is something wrong?" Cindy asked as she served herself some salad. "It's not Mother, is it?"

"No, no," Nicole hastened to reassure her. "It's just that I called the catering shop twice this afternoon and I got the answering machine both times. Where could Carol be?"

Cindy relaxed. "Probably had a delivery to make or something. Don't worry about it." Both girls knew that their mother's assistant had always been reliable.

"But I looked at Mother's calendar and they didn't have anything scheduled for today."

"So she's out buying groceries. Relax, Nicole. You can talk to her tomorrow."

Cindy, in no great hurry to start their self-appointed tasks at the shop, seemed unconcerned. Nicole shook her head.

"I just hope nothing's wrong," she murmured as sounds from the hall heralded the return of Mollie and Mr. Lewis. "Don't tell Mother, we have to keep her from worrying."

"Don't overreact, Nicole. What could possibly be wrong?" Cindy said, reaching for the tray of sandwiches.

But Nicole continued to frown.

Chapter 3

When they reached the hospital and made their way to Mrs. Lewis's room, the girls were delighted to find that their mother, though slightly pale and looking tired, greeted them cheerfully.

"Mom, you look great!" Cindy cried, almost dropping the vase of flowers she was carrying as she hurried over to give her mother a big hug.

Laura Lewis smiled. "I think that's a slight exaggeration," she said, "but thank you anyhow."

Mollie, ever the worrywart, regarded her mother's pale face and dark-circled eyes gravely. "Do you feel okay?"

"I'm just fine, Mollie," her mother assured her, giving the youngest Lewis a warm embrace. "The nurses are being very sweet, and I'm really quite comfortable, considering."

"Considering that she's just out of surgery," Richard Lewis pointed out, leaning over to kiss his wife. "You can't expect her to be ready to go dancing."

"Not just yet," their mother agreed, laughing. "How are you, Nicole?"

Nicole, last in line for a hug, wasn't aware that her soft blue eyes revealed more of the past twenty-four hours' worry than she would have wished. She smiled for her mother's benefit. "*Très bien,* now that you're okay. I made dinner for everyone."

"And a late breakfast," Cindy added, determined that Nicole should receive full credit. "And it was all delicious."

"I'm sure it was," Mrs. Lewis said. "Thank you, Nicole. I'm sure I can count on you all—on all of my girls—to help out at home until I'm back on my feet."

Nicole exchanged a significant look with her sisters. "You don't have to worry about a thing at home *or* at work, Mother. We're going to spend our vacation helping out at the shop. We just want you to concentrate on getting well!"

The other girls assented loudly, while Mrs. Lewis looked startled. "I don't want you to give up your whole vacation, girls. Carol is very capable, and in a few days I'll be able to—"

"Now Laura," Mr. Lewis interrupted. "I've already talked to the doctor, and he said—"

While their parents argued, Nicole whispered

to Cindy, "You see. I told you she would want to get right back to work."

Cindy nodded. "Don't worry. We'll keep her away from the shop."

"Don't forget about me," Mollie put in, her voice indignant. "I can help, too!"

Cindy rolled her eyes, and Mollie bristled, but Nicole hurried to play peacemaker. "Not now, *enfants*. Not in front of Mother. We'll all pitch in. Now shut up!"

"Of course I'll listen to the doctor," Mrs. Lewis was saying to her husband. "Although I do hate for the girls to give up all their vacation plans."

"You're more important than a few days' vacation, *Maman*," Nicole pointed out. At that she received a fond smile from her mother.

"You're all very sweet. I have the most wonderful family in the whole world."

The look she gave them was reward enough to take away all their regrets. Cindy even forgot about the surfing parties she would have to miss.

Richard Lewis grinned. "Be careful, you're going to give us all swelled heads."

Then Cindy began to recount her afternoon at the DMV and her near disaster. She showed her mother the comic license plate that Duffy had substituted for the real one, and when Laura Lewis laughed, Cindy laughed, too.

"It's cute, isn't it?" Cindy said. "I think I'll put it up in my bedroom. But I could have killed Duffy this afternoon. I'll have to think of *some* way to get even."

Then Mollie told their mother about Winston and the cats, who Mollie could tell were already missing the lady of the house. "Smokey keeps going into your bedroom to look for you; honest, I think she knows something's up. And Winston looks positively woebegone."

Mrs. Lewis smiled. "I'm sure you can keep his spirits up until I get home."

The visiting hours passed swiftly until the sound of a bell from the hallway warned them it was time to leave. Richard Lewis gave his wife one more kiss. "Sleep well," he told her.

"I'm sure that won't be a problem," Laura Lewis answered. "Keep the home fires burning."

"We will," they chorused, while Mollie murmured to herself, "It's too warm for a fire!"

"Dummy!" Cindy groaned. "It's just an expression."

They argued all the way home.

Nicole got up early Tuesday morning, in time to share a pot of coffee with her dad before he left for work. Then she dressed and did her hair, glad that she hadn't scheduled any modeling assignments over the spring break. When Cindy returned from her early morning jog, surprised to see her sister already up, Nicole was phoning the shop again.

"Still no answer," Nicole told her. "*Mon dieu,* Cindy. I just know something's wrong."

"You worry too much," Cindy said as she went to the pantry to get out the cereal. "Maybe she went to the hospital to visit Mom."

"Carol doesn't even know that Mother's in the hospital, *idiot.* No one told her. Hurry up and eat," Nicole said. "I'll get Mollie up, and we'll drive down to the shop."

"How are you going to get in?"

"Mother's extra key is on the key rack in the kitchen; she won't mind if I borrow it."

Mollie, still happily somnolent, was not easy to rouse. "It's too early, Nicole!"

"It's almost nine," her sister said firmly. "We're going down to the catering shop. If you meant what you said about helping Mother, get yourself out of bed."

Still grumbling, Mollie managed to push herself out from under the bedcovers and pull on the first pair of jeans and T-shirt that she touched. Who cared how she looked if she had to work all day? On the other hand, who knew what gorgeous guy might wander into the shop? "Although, knowing Nicole, I'll end up with all the grubby jobs," Mollie said to Cinders as the lanky cat wound himself around her ankles. Hopping around the room as she tried to pull on her jeans, Mollie stepped on the cat, who yowled indignantly.

"It's your own fault, get out of the way," Mollie said. Leaving her cluttered bedroom without a second glance, she headed for the bathroom to put on her makeup.

When she got downstairs, Nicole was waiting impatiently.

"What took you so long?"

"I had to make myself presentable," Mollie told her primly. "What's for breakfast?"

"Grab a piece of toast, and hurry up. I want to get started."

Mollie, relinquishing visions of one of Nicole's fluffy omelets, sighed.

Eventually they all crowded into the family station wagon, Cindy eagerly claiming the keys, and headed for the catering shop.

Sure enough, the small shop appeared deserted. Cindy parked the car in the back of the building, and Nicole let them in with their mother's key.

"I don't understand," Nicole murmured. "Where could Carol be?"

"Maybe she's sick," Cindy suggested. "Did you try her home phone?"

"Twice, no answer." Nicole headed for the front of the shop to check the mail while the two girls looked over the familiar kitchen with its long gleaming counters and commercial ovens. Everything was neat and clean as usual. Their mother's efficiency was as evident here as at home.

Nicole frowned as she came back with a handful of envelopes. She glanced through the stack of mail.

"Mostly bills—oh!"

"What is it?" Mollie asked.

"*Mon dieu,* a special delivery letter—from Carol!" Nicole hesitated for a moment, then made up her mind and began to rip open the envelope.

"You can't open that!" Cindy sounded outraged. "That's for Mom."

"Unusual circumstances call for unusual responses," Nicole answered, somewhat pompously.

"And what Frenchman said that?" Cindy was unimpressed.

"I forget. But if something's wrong with Carol—suppose she's had an accident—we have to find out before Mother does. We're supposed to keep her from worrying, *n'est-ce pas?*"

Nicole, scanning the short letter, gasped.

"What is it?" the other two girls demanded.

" 'Dear Laura,' " Nicole read aloud, " 'I tried to call you, but no one was home'—must have been yesterday when we were all out back. I told you to bring the phone out on the patio, Mollie."

Mollie looked guilty, but Cindy urged, "Go on!"

Nicole continued to read. " 'Jim received orders for an immediate transfer, some kind of foul-up at the Vienna plant that only their very best trouble-shooter engineer can correct, he had to catch a plane Sunday night for Europe. We've been talking about marriage for months, and I couldn't make a decision'—oh, dear." Nicole said, worried. "This is rather personal."

"Keep reading," Cindy insisted. "We have to find out where Carol is."

"And who's Jim?" Mollie wondered aloud.

"Carol's boyfriend," Nicole told her. "They've been going out for almost two years." She went back to the letter. " 'I was so upset. Then Jim asked me to go with him. Laura, what else could I do? We're stopping in Las Vegas to be married, then we can squeeze in one night in Paris!' " Nicole paused, overcome by the thought of a honeymoon, no matter how brief, in the City of Light.

But Cindy urged, "Go on—"

" 'I'm terribly sorry to leave you with no notice, but I'm sure you'll understand, considering the circumstances. Jim is so wonderful, and I'm so happy—but you've heard all this before! I sent a note to Maureen asking her to fill in at the shop until you can hire a permanent replacement. Forgive me for the abrupt departure, and wish us all the best.' "

Nicole lowered the sheet of paper, and the girls stared at each other blankly. "Carol's gone—she's in Europe by now!"

"What about Maureen?"

"There's a postcard here," Nicole suddenly realized. She turned it over and read aloud, " 'Dear Carol and Laura, Sorry to turn you down, but I've just accepted a new post in Sacramento. Maureen.' "

Even Nicole looked bleak, and Mollie wailed, "No one is coming!"

"Mom will have a fit," Cindy murmured.

Nicole visibly pulled herself together. "You two

listen—Mother is *not* to be told, do you understand? She'd get up out of her hospital bed if she knew that Carol was gone, and we can't have her risking her health!" Nicole's voice was so fierce that the younger girls trembled.

"But, Nicole, we can't run this place alone!"

"*Mais oui,* we have to," Nicole told them. "We can't let Mother's reputation suffer. What would her clients think if she doesn't fulfill her contracts? We won't accept any new jobs, but we have to take care of the ones she's already accepted. It won't be so bad, really. I *can* cook, you know, and with you two to carry and clean—"

"Oh, great," Cindy murmured. Nicole rounded on her sister fiercely.

"*Mon dieu,* do you want to help Mother or not?"

"Of course I do," Cindy snapped. "But I didn't know I'd have to work for *you*."

Nicole recovered herself enough to grin. "I won't be bossy. Well—" She paused. "I'll try not to be, anyhow. And this is for Mother."

"I know, I know," Cindy said with a sigh. "We'll do it, Nicole. We don't have much choice."

"We can do it," Mollie decided. "What can be so hard about running a catering business?"

Chapter 4

*T*he Lewis sisters stood in the center of the large kitchen and looked at each other, a little awed by the enormity of the responsibilities they were about to assume.

"Where do we start, Nicole?" Mollie asked, her expression slightly apprehensive.

Nicole, trying to appear in control of the situation, swallowed nervously before replying. "I'll check Mother's calendar to see what's coming up this week; you and Cindy take stock of the pantry and freezer to see how much food we have on hand."

Mollie nodded, and Cindy, always impatient, had already moved toward the big commercial freezer at the back of the room.

Nicole, pleased that she had come up with a

sensible answer, went to the desk to check her mother's appointment book. To her relief, she found that only one gourmet picnic had been booked for this week, but the coming weekend held a garden wedding and a large reception for the Santa Barbara Fine Arts Committee. And the following week there was an important luncheon for the city council scheduled.

"Mon dieu!" Nicole murmured to herself. Would they be able to carry this off? They had to—they couldn't ruin the reputation their mother had worked years to build up. Nicole mumbled a fervent prayer under her breath as she began to check the menus her mother had planned. Could she make all these recipes on her own? If not, she hoped their clients would forgive a few substitutions.

She could hear the two girls in the back. "Gosh, it's cold in here," Mollie exclaimed. "Cindy, don't you dare lock me in!"

"Cindy!" Nicole yelled over her shoulder. "Stop horsing around."

"Who, me?" Cindy, looking entirely too innocent, reappeared, followed by a mutinous Mollie. "I remember when a certain little sister locked me and Grant into a closet at school—"

"That was for your own good," Mollie protested. "You were about to lose one of the best catches at Vista High—just because you were feeling overly independent! And anyhow, there was no danger of you freezing to death."

"Cut it out, you two," Nicole said impatiently. "What did you find?"

Cindy, recalled to a sense of duty, answered soberly, "I don't know what's coming up, Nicole, but this place doesn't look too well stocked to me. The refrigerator is almost empty of fruits and fresh vegetables."

Nicole tried not to panic as she composed a logical response. "Fresh foods don't keep very long; Mother usually reorders at the beginning of the week."

She continued to search through the neat collection of folders on her mother's desk and was rewarded with one marked SUPPLIERS.

"Here, Cindy. As soon as I make out a list of the ingredients we'll need for the next few days, you sit down with the phone and order what we need from mother's usual suppliers. Be professional, remember, no joking around."

"I can be as businesslike as anyone," Cindy retorted, ignoring Mollie's baleful glance. "Most of the time."

Nicole, who was still compiling recipes and lists of ingredients, ignored her.

Mollie drifted over to the cupboards and checked the neatly labeled canisters and boxes, wondering just how many chocolate chip cookies she could mix up with fifty pounds of flour.

Unfortunately Nicole soon cut this agreeable daydream short.

"Cindy, here's the list. Get busy with the telephone. Mollie, where are you?"

"Right here."

"We have a gourmet dinner for two scheduled for tomorrow. I'd love to make a soufflé, but unfortunately it's a picnic dinner, so the food has to be portable. Let me see, vichyssoise should be made ahead of time. Mollie, chop some green onions for me."

"I hate chopping onions," Mollie protested.

"Mollie!" Stared down by Nicole's best older-sister look, the younger girl gave in.

"Oh, all right," she said, her tone sulky as she turned toward the refrigerator.

"Don't forget to wash your hands first," Nicole added. "It'd really be awful if we made some poor soul ill."

"I'm not a baby, Nicole," Mollie grumbled.

Cindy, who had finally gotten the right person on the line, covered the receiver with one hand while she yelled to her sister, "Nicole, how many mushrooms?"

Nicole, looking back over the menus for the next week, computed hurriedly in her head. How many mushrooms did those little baskets hold? Probably a pound.

"Nicole?"

"Six—no, make that ten boxes," Nicole answered, thinking to herself, Better to have too many than to run out in the middle of a recipe. Then she added, "Cindy, is that the fresh fruit and vegetable man? We need bananas, too, for half a dozen pies."

"How many?" was the instant reply.

"Use your head," Nicole snapped. "I can't make all the decisions."

Cindy, aggrieved, stuck out her tongue at her sister before turning back to the telephone.

When Cindy hung up the phone, Nicole looked up from her recipes to say, "If you're through, Cindy, why don't you start some fresh bread for the gourmet picnic tomorrow." Nicole, ashamed of her momentary loss of patience, tried to speak pleasantly, but Cindy still glowered.

"Here's the recipe; get one of the big bowls from the cupboard; all the ingredients should be there."

Cindy glanced quickly over the printed sheet, then began to pull out canisters of flour, sugar, and salt. The shortening took a little longer to locate. She began to measure the flour.

The counter soon took on the aspect of a mountain slope in winter, lightly dusted with snow. Despite this, Cindy began to enjoy her task. "Knead well," the instructions said. Cindy, who could remember her mother saying that making bread was good exercise, pounded the pliant dough with enthusiasm.

"Don't pulverize it, Cindy," Nicole said, coming to look over her shoulder. "It's got to rise, remember. How much yeast did you put in?"

"Yeast?" Cindy suddenly lost her zest, and the

guilty expression on her face made Nicole draw her brows together into a stern frown.

"You didn't forget the yeast? Cindy, *mon dieu,* how could you?"

"No big deal." Cindy tried to excuse her slight oversight. "I'll stick it in now."

"You can't, *idiot.* The yeast goes in first! You'll have to throw out the whole thing and start over."

Cindy, who had been quite proud of her first pan of bread dough, felt foolish.

"I'll do it myself this time," Nicole decided. "But you clean up this mess first, you've got flour over half the kitchen. Then you can put the artichokes in to boil."

"We don't have any artichokes." Cindy, who was fast losing patience with her autocratic sister, was quite pleased to point out this oversight.

"Why didn't you order them when you were on the phone, *idiot*?"

"Because you didn't tell me to, remember? You're the one who was supposed to compile the list of ingredients. And if you call me idiot in that French accent one more time, I'm going to cram this broom down your throat!"

Cindy lifted the broom to emphasize her threat, and the two girls glared angrily at each other. The impasse was broken by a large sniff from behind them.

Nicole, guiltily reminded of her responsibility as the eldest, recovered her poise first.

"Mollie," she exclaimed, "don't cry, *ma petite.* Cindy and I aren't really angry at each other."

"I don't care about that," Mollie wailed. "It's these onions!"

Nicole hurried over to the cutting board by the big sink to inspect Mollie's labors.

"Mollie, I said *green* onions, not these big yellow ones! They'll ruin the taste of the vichyssoise."

"Well, I didn't know." Mollie sobbed. "What do I do now?"

Nicole sighed. "Store them in a sealable plastic box and put them in the crisper. Maybe we can use them in something else. Then let me show you what green onions look like."

Nicole led Mollie to the refrigerator and pointed out the correct vegetables. Then she gave Cindy money for the artichokes and dispatched the middle Lewis to the nearest supermarket.

"Make sure they're fresh," was her parting cry.

"As if I'd know a fresh artichoke if it bit me," Cindy grumbled. But at least she got to drive the car alone. She still hadn't gotten over her thrill at receiving her license and becoming a bona fide driver. She pulled out into the street with ease, proud of her increasing confidence, and headed for the supermarket.

The rest of the afternoon went comparatively smoothly. Cindy returned from her errands and was allowed to knead the new batch of bread dough before setting it aside to rise. Nicole made the shrimp salad that would be used to stuff the artichokes and whipped up a delectable chocolate cheesecake that she kept from her hungry sisters with great difficulty.

"Just a taste, Nicole," Mollie pleaded. "You want to know how good it is, don't you?"

"It's delicious," Nicole answered heartlessly. "I already tasted it."

"You could have made an extra one while you were at it," Cindy grumbled.

"I did, but I'm saving it. We might need an extra dessert this weekend." Nicole's tone was firm.

"What are *we* going to have for dinner?" Mollie sounded plaintive, and Nicole relented slightly, even though the thought of more cooking after a day of culinary labors didn't appeal to her.

"I'll think of something. Dad has to eat, too, *n'est-ce pas?*"

They had almost finished cleaning up the kitchen when there was a sudden honking from behind the store.

"What on earth is that?"

"I bet it's our deliveries." Cindy suddenly remembered the orders she had placed with the supplier earlier in the day. "I'll stick the mushrooms and fruit in the fridge. Then let's get home and get our own dinner. I'm starved."

She hurried to open the back door. A tall man holding a clipboard stood in front of a large truck.

"Movable Feasts?"

"That's us," Cindy said. "You have our mushrooms?"

The man nodded. "Ten crates. Where do you want them?"

"Just set them inside," Cindy said blithely, unaware that behind her Nicole's knees almost gave way and she had to grasp the counter to stay erect.

"Crates?" Nicole managed to gasp. "Cindy, I never said *crates*."

Cindy, her eyes popping as the driver began to unload large wooden crates crammed full of fresh mushrooms, was momentarily speechless. The large boxes took up most of the floor space of the big kitchen and surely held enough mushrooms to feed most of Santa Barbara.

"Uh, are you sure that's our order?" Cindy said.

"That's what it says, kid." The man held out his clipboard to show her the paper. "Where's the lady in charge, anyhow?"

"She's not in the shop just now."

"Sign here," the man said.

Cindy and Nicole exchanged anguished glances. "I don't suppose you could return some of these?" Nicole asked weakly.

"No returns, you know our policy." The driver began to look impatient.

Cindy, shrugging in resignation, scrawled her name on the paper.

"I'll leave the bananas outside," the driver said as he headed out the door.

Nicole tried to swallow. "You don't mean—how many bananas do we have?"

"Ten crates, what else."

"Mon dieu," Nicole muttered, while behind them, Mollie dissolved into a fit of laughter.

Chapter 5

*A*fter all the crates of bananas had been lugged inside the front door of the shop, and the freshly baked bread had been put away, the girls made it home just before their dad. Nicole went straight to work in the kitchen, and when Richard Lewis walked through the back door, a savory aroma hung in the air. He sniffed contentedly.

"Something smells good."

"Mushroom soup," Nicole told him.

Behind her, Mollie, who was setting the table, tried her best to swallow an attack of giggles. She succeeded only in disguising her slightly hysterical laughter with a fit of coughing.

"Getting a cold, Mollie?" their father asked.

"I'm fine," Mollie said, red-faced from trying to avoid another outburst of laughter.

"It's just a little supper." Nicole ignored her youngest sister. "Mushroom soup, fresh bread, and fruit salad."

"With lots of bananas," Mollie added, and, to her dad's puzzlement, dissolved into another fit of giggling.

"That's fine. I want to eat quickly, then visit your mother. Did you girls go down to the hospital this afternoon?"

"No." Nicole began to ladle the soup into bowls. "We were busy at the shop."

"Was Carol glad to have your help?" Mr. Lewis asked, as he shrugged off his jacket and loosened his tie.

"Uh, sure, I think." Nicole faltered a moment, very glad that her dad's attention had already been diverted by the middle Lewis's appearance in the doorway.

"How's the new driver?"

"Great." Cindy grinned at him. "Nicole let me drive to the shop. I'm getting really good, Dad."

Mr. Lewis chuckled at Cindy's unabashed pride in her new skill.

"Just remember to be a cautious driver, and always wear your seat belt."

"Dinner's ready," Cindy said quickly, afraid that a full-blown lecture would follow. "Let's eat so we can go see Mom."

Nicole's soup was thick and delicious, and Cindy claimed part of the credit for the savory fresh-baked bread.

"It was my kneading that made it so light," she explained, ignoring Nicole's dry glance.

After a short visit with their mother, they returned home, and all three girls retired to bed early. Mr. Lewis raised his brows as his daughters headed upstairs. Such early bedtime during school vacation were unusual. "Carol must have worked you three pretty hard today."

Nicole, feeling guilty, nodded, and the two younger girls pretended not to hear. At the top of the stairs, Cindy whispered to her older sister. "What are we going to do with all those mushrooms and bananas?"

Nicole, feeling incredibly weary, shrugged. "*Je ne sais pas.* Who knows? I'll try to think of something."

Cindy, wishing that she had nothing more to worry about than how high the surf would be tomorrow, went to bed and dreamed that she was drowning in a sea of mushrooms.

The next morning Nicole roused Mollie, and all three girls were at the shop before nine. Nicole took out her checklist for the afternoon picnic and began to finish her preparations. She put the artichokes on to boil, then stuffed them with the shrimp salad when they were done.

"Mollie, start washing and drying these mushrooms," Nicole ordered. "We'll put away as many as we can possibly use fresh, and package more for the freezer."

"Can you freeze mushrooms?" Mollie asked, wrinkling her nose at the thought of the huge task ahead of her.

"I really don't know, but we'll try," Nicole admitted. "Cindy, start preparing the picnic basket—wineglasses, silver, the best tablecloth."

"This is for a picnic?" Cindy demanded.

"It's a *gourmet* picnic," Nicole explained, sounding lofty. Her sister made a face but did as she was told.

"Drat," Nicole said, a little later, as she bumped into a crate for the tenth time. "Mollie, how many mushrooms have you put away?"

"I've filled two crispers and put two-dozen bags into the freezer. I've hardly made a dent, Nicole." Mollie looked tired already. "There's an *awful* lot of mushrooms here."

"What are we going to do? We've got to get rid of these crates!" Nicole looked worn-out. Her usually sleek French braid had loosened, and wispy tendrils of soft brown hair hung down around her face.

"You're telling me," Cindy said. "But how? We can't just throw them out. Mom has to pay for all this."

"Don't remind me." Nicole groaned, feeling responsible for the goof-up. "We can't just take a loss on all this."

Mollie looked bewildered, and Cindy explained

in a patronizing tone, "In business, that means that you've lost money—gone in the hole."

"A canyon would be more like it," Nicole said. *"Mon dieu,* who's that?"

A slender young man in a blue jacket and neat tie had entered through the front door of the shop. Nicole, trying fruitlessly to push her hair back into place, hurried to greet him.

The stranger stared in surprise at the crates of bananas that crowded the small front room.

"A new shipment," Nicole explained weakly. "Can I help you?"

"I'm James Whitney. I ordered a gourmet picnic for two?"

For a moment Nicole thought she might scream. "You're too early. I mean, wasn't it scheduled for two o'clock?"

"Yes, it was," the young man hastened to reassure her. "I just wanted to make sure that everything is set."

"Why wouldn't it be?" Nicole sounded almost belligerent. Did he know that no one was in the shop but three teenagers?

But when the young man grinned nervously, Nicole relaxed.

"No reason. I mean, your reputation is excellent; that's why I chose this shop. At least, you're not Mrs. Lewis, are you?"

Nicole tensed again. "That's my mother; she's not in at the moment."

"But everything's ready for this afternoon?"

"Of course."

"Thank goodness." The young man paused to wipe his brow, and Nicole's curiosity could no longer be contained.

"This must be a very important meeting; is it for business?"

"Oh, no, just the opposite." James, who seemed eager to explain his nervousness, drew a small jeweler's box out of his inside pocket. "It's for my girlfriend. I want exactly the right moment to propose."

He flipped open the small box and allowed Nicole to see an impressive diamond ring. A slight gasp behind them alerted Nicole to an eavesdropper, and she turned around and caught a glimpse of Mollie peeking around the inner door. With a frown and a wave of her hand to shoo Mollie away, Nicole turned back to face the young man.

"Everything has got to be perfect, you see. I—I'm a little nervous about this."

"I'm sure your girlfriend will be delighted," Nicole assured him, hoping fervently that it was true. He looked nice enough, if a bit on edge.

"I hope so." His voice sounded wistful. "This is my second try. I arranged a gondola ride in Venice the first time, and I meant to ask her while we rode down the canals."

Nicole, familiar with the California coastal community whose canals had prompted its name, nodded. "Weren't you able to—I mean, did something go wrong?"

"The gondola sprang a leak," James told her. "It didn't turn out to be the most romantic experience."

A stifled burst of giggling from the kitchen made Nicole say loudly, *"Mon dieu,* how dreadful. Don't worry about a thing, Mr. Whitney. This afternoon will go smoothly. We guarantee a serene atmosphere for your picnic. Where would you like it to take place?"

"That's what I came to tell you," James said. "Maybe up above the beach, on Shore Line Road. But"—he grinned sheepishly—"no crowds, okay? We need a little privacy."

Or this poor girl will never get her engagement ring, Nicole thought to herself while she nodded. "We'll select an appropriate site. Don't worry."

As soon as the door swung shut behind him, Mollie danced out of the kitchen. "Isn't that the most romantic story you ever heard?"

Nicole turned on her little sister fiercely. "The next time I catch you eavesdropping, I'm going to strangle you, Mollie!"

"But I couldn't help it. What a story!" Mollie argued. "Wait till I tell—"

"Don't you dare!" Nicole's anger grew. "We have a responsibility here, Mollie. Like a—a lawyer, we have to protect our clients. You can't tell the whole school about Mr. Whitney's private life!"

"Oh, all right," Mollie consented. "But I still think it's terribly romantic."

"What about the mushrooms?" Nicole brought

her sister back to more mundane matters, and Mollie's blissful expression faded rapidly.

"Don't ask me to do any more mushrooms! Honestly, we can't fill up the whole freezer, Nicole."

"I suppose not," Nicole agreed as they returned to the kitchen.

"Forget the mushrooms for a minute," Cindy said. "I've got the hamper ready. The champagne is in the cooler. All we need now is the food."

"I need a few minutes to finish," Nicole said. "We can't be late. You and Mollie put the table and chairs into the back of the station wagon. Find a good spot and set up the table, then come back for the food. Just be sure to find a good location. Remember, he wants privacy."

"Right." Cindy, happy to have another excuse to drive, grabbed the keys and her denim bag with her precious license and headed for the car.

"Wait for me," Mollie yelled, anxious to get away from the crates of mushrooms.

They drove along the bluffs overlooking the beach until Cindy spotted an isolated spot that looked appropriately romantic. She pulled the station wagon off the road and said to Mollie, "Wait here while I take a look."

They were high over the Santa Barbara beaches, far enough out of town so that the vista was free of vacationers. Cindy walked to the edge of the sandy spur and looked down at the waves rolling into the beach. She let out a loud sigh.

What she'd give to be down there right now. But this was for Mom, she reminded herself, and pulled her thoughts back to the business at hand.

She walked along the sandy cliff until she located what looked like a perfect place. Then she noticed a faded sign proclaiming, DANGER, UNSTABLE AREA.

Cindy shook her head. Too bad. The table would have to go back closer to the road. She gave one last wistful glance toward the beach—the salt smell of the breeze alone made her homesick for her surfboard—and pulled off her jacket, tossing it over the small sign.

She walked back to the car and pulled the station wagon up to the spot she had selected. Opening the tailgate, she called to Mollie, "Give me a hand with the folding table, please."

Between them, they carted the table and chairs back to the selected site and set up the table on the sandy ground.

"We're running out of time, Cindy," Mollie warned, glancing at her watch.

"I know. You stay here and set the table; the tablecloth and stuff are in this bag. Nicole wanted a rose in a bud vase on the table; don't forget that. For *ambiance,* she said."

"Wouldn't salt and pepper hold down the cloth just as well?" Mollie asked as the sea breeze ruffled her long blond hair.

"No, dummy. The rose is to set the mood." Cindy shook her head at her sister, who looked unperturbed. "I'll go back to collect the food and tell Nicole where to send the lovebirds."

Cindy jumped back into the station wagon, and the car pulled away, spewing sand. Mollie watched her go, then turned back to the table.

"Left with the dirty work, as usual," she said to herself. "I could do a better job than either of those two. How come all I ever get to do is follow orders?"

Mollie looked at the bare table critically. "They can't even see the beach from here," she noted. "What was Cindy thinking of?"

She walked closer to the edge of the sandy cliff and nodded wisely. "This would be much better; we've got to get that poor guy to propose this time."

It wasn't easy to move the table by herself, but Mollie, with great determination, finally did it. After she had placed the table and two chairs closer to the cliff edge, she covered the table with the linen cloth and set out silverware and napkins. Last, she poured water from a thermos into the crystal bud vase and took the single flawless rosebud from its box.

"Perfect," she told herself happily, after placing the flower on the table. "Won't Nicole be proud of me?"

She walked back to the edge of the road to watch for Cindy's return. Soon she spotted the familiar station wagon, and Cindy pulled to a stop at the side of the pavement.

"Doesn't it look nice?" Mollie asked, eager for praise.

"Terrific—hey, why did you move the table?" Cindy, pausing as she lifted out the heavy basket of food, frowned at her sister.

Offended, Mollie answered, "There's a much better view from here. What's that?"

A sudden rumbling made both girls start, and they whirled around just in time to watch the sandy spur collapse beneath the weight of the portable furniture. The table, with its lovely setting, slipped down, down, and out of sight.

Mollie shrieked, grabbing her sister's arm. Cindy groaned and shut her eyes.

When the dust had settled, they approached the edge of the cliff with the greatest caution and saw the pieces of their picnic set half buried in the sand below.

"I didn't mean to, Cindy." Mollie sobbed.

"Didn't you read the sign?"

"What sign?"

"Oh, never mind." Cindy shook her head.

"Can we go back and get another table?"

"That was the only one we had. Mother doesn't keep many on hand; she rents them when she needs more than one, and the rental shop needs twenty-four hours' notice."

"What are we going to do? The courting couple will be here any minute!"

"I know, I know," Cindy muttered. "We'll just have to apologize and postpone their dinner."

"We can't," Mollie cried. "That poor girl will never get her ring!"

"So?" Cindy glared at her romantic little sister. "What do you suggest, shrimp?"

Mollie took a deep breath. "Cindy! I have an idea."

"What?" Cindy looked skeptical, but this was no time to argue.

"I need a telephone."

"There's one just down the road."

"Hurry!"

Cindy drove to the public phone and waited while Mollie made a phone call, trying to hear what her little sister was saying so urgently into the phone. But all she could catch was a word or two. Completely mystified, Cindy waited for the youngest Lewis to jump back into the car.

But Mollie still didn't explain. "Back to the bluff," she ordered.

They drove back to the bluff and pulled off to the side of the road.

"Okay, what gives?" Cindy demanded. The sound of a car approaching made her turn pale beneath her freckles. "Oh no!"

A small sedan pulled up behind the station wagon. Mollie and Cindy looked at each other, then at the driver, recognizing the young man from the shop. Mollie couldn't help taking a quick look at the young woman in the passenger seat, a demure-looking brunette with a sweet face, perfect for the timid young man, Mollie decided.

Then he rolled down the window and spoke to her, and his question jerked her back to the problem at hand.

"Are you—are you from Movable Feasts? Where's our picnic?"

"Uh—" Mollie's mind went completely blank. She looked from the customer's concerned face to her watch. How long had it been since her call? "It's—I mean, we're almost—"

Her stuttering would have continued indefinitely, but the sound of another car on the quiet road made both of them turn. To Mollie's relief, a sleek white Rolls-Royce convertible pulled up behind them. A uniformed driver jumped out and removed his cap with a theatrical flourish.

"Mr. James Whitney?"

"Yes," the surprised young man said.

"Everything is prepared for your gourmet picnic for two—served in a classic Rolls on a scenic coast road."

"Well." The young man glanced at the vintage car with appreciation, then smiled at his lady friend. "This is service, I must say."

The driver helped the two into the back of the grand old car, then took the picnic basket and wine cooler from Mollie with a private wink.

Mollie grinned back and watched them drive away. Hardly had the automobile disappeared when Cindy turned to her sister, her expression a comic mixture of bewilderment and exasperation.

"Okay, how did you manage that—on such short

notice, too? And who's the guy with the fake English accent?"

Mollie giggled. "He did sound like the perfect English butler, didn't he?"

"Mollie!"

Mollie backed away as Cindy approached, her expression threatening. "Okay! That's Heather's cousin. He's a college student, but he drives one of his dad's antique cars in his spare time to earn money."

Cindy regarded her sister with rare respect. "Gosh. What's he studying?"

"Acting, of course." Mollie giggled again, then sobered. "Does Nicole have to know what happened?"

"How else do you think we can explain the missing furniture? Or the bill from the limo service?" Cindy asked dryly. "Come on, let's drive down to the beach and see if any of our stuff can be salvaged."

"Okay," Mollie agreed. "And let's take our time."

"Afraid to face Nicole, huh?"

"No." Mollie shuddered. "Tired of washing mushrooms!"

Chapter 6

*W*hen they returned to the catering shop, Cindy and Mollie had salvaged one of the folding chairs, but the other chair and the table, bent and twisted by the fall, were beyond repair. The fragile vase had been smashed into dozens of tiny fragments and the linen tablecloth ripped. So they walked into the shop very quietly.

To their surprise, Nicole was humming happily.

"Why are you in such a good mood?" Cindy asked.

"I found a way to dispose of the mushrooms," Nicole told them.

"How?" Cindy demanded, while Mollie breathed a sigh of relief.

"I read in the local news that the Women's Club is holding a charity auction tomorrow. I called, and they're willing to accept the mush-rooms. Those ladies are all great cooks. And since it's for charity, Mother can use the donation as a tax write-off, so it won't be a total loss."

"Great," Cindy agreed.

"All we have to do is separate the mushrooms into small bags," Nicole continued.

Mollie groaned. "I knew it was too good to be true!"

"Come on, let's get to work. I promised we'd have them delivered by four o'clock. Oh, how did the picnic go?"

"Fine," Cindy said hastily, throwing a warning glance at the youngest Lewis. Time enough for details later; let Nicole enjoy her good spirits for a while.

Nicole handed them both a stack of small white bags, and they went to work.

"I don't suppose they wanted any bananas?" Cindy asked.

Nicole shot her a dirty look. "Bite your tongue," she snapped.

Mollie, elbow-deep in mushrooms, sighed.

After the girls delivered the mushrooms, they drove home and found their father in the kitchen, glancing through the mail.

"Another hard day, girls?" he asked, throwing them a searching glance. "I think I'll tell Carol that she's working you too hard."

"Mais non!" Nicole straightened her sagging

shoulders with effort. "We enjoy it, Dad. And we want to help Mother out, you know that."

"Okay," Richard Lewis agreed. "I'm proud of you for wanting to help. But forget about making dinner tonight, we'll order in a pizza. How's that?"

"Sounds great, Dad," Cindy agreed, fending off a playful Winston.

"I know Cindy and I want the Supreme, and Nicole likes pepperoni. What about you, Mollie?" their dad asked, heading for the telephone.

"Anything but mushrooms," Mollie said, and, unaware of her dad's puzzled glance, headed upstairs for the shower. She felt as if she were about to turn into a fungus herself.

After a shower and a couple of phone calls, Mollie felt much more like her usual bubbly self. The savory smell of pizza drew her quickly down the stairs, where she joined the rest of the family at the table, eating pizza off paper plates.

"Guess what, Cindy," Mollie whispered, throwing a secret grin at her sister. "Heather told me that her cousin said that James's girlfriend left the picnic with the ring on her finger." She took a large slice of pepperoni pizza and bit into the thick crust.

"Good for him," Cindy whispered back.

Nicole stood up and began to collect the plates. "Hurry up, Mollie. Hospital visiting hours start in twenty minutes."

Mollie, her mouth full, gave a muffled protest

and grabbed the rest of the pizza before Nicole could take it away.

Mrs. Lewis, who appeared stronger every day, smiled at her family when they arrived at the hospital. After a few minutes' quiet conversation with her husband, she turned to the girls, who had been admiring the flowers sent by relatives and friends.

"I understand you're all working very hard at the shop," Laura Lewis said.

Nicole nodded, wishing she didn't feel quite so guilty. They *were* working hard; that part certainly wasn't a deception.

"I rather thought Carol would have called," Mrs. Lewis began, and Nicole gave a sudden start.

"I forgot. She told me to send you her best regards, and tell you she's thinking of you, but she's been too busy to come visit," Nicole improvised.

"Goodness, we're not *that* busy, are we?" Mrs. Lewis looked concerned, and Cindy tried to help out her sister.

"It's just that we—she—everyone wants the shop to be run perfectly while you're away."

Laura Lewis relaxed. "Well, she needn't worry. I have complete trust in her, especially since she has such devoted assistants."

The three girls exchanged glances, then Mollie began to tell her mother about a terrific outfit she'd seen last week at a local boutique. For once the other two were glad to listen to Mollie's chatter, anything to get their mother's thoughts away from the shop.

The next morning, a balmy, beautiful day that made Cindy long for the beach, found the girls back in the catering shop.

"At least those dratted mushrooms are history," Mollie pointed out.

Nicole nodded. It was a relief to have room to work in the kitchen again, but the front room was still full of crates of bananas.

"Do I get to do something interesting today?" Mollie asked hopefully.

"You can sweep the floor," Nicole told her. "And then start slicing bananas."

"Nicole!"

But her sister's stern look forced Mollie toward the broom closet.

"I'll put out some recipes: Banana pudding, banana cream pie, and banana cheesecake. You two can work on them. What we don't use for the wedding can be served at the arts reception Sunday."

"Banana cheesecake?" Cindy hooted.

Nicole's glance was baleful. "Trust me."

"And what are you going to be doing, Your Highness, while we slave over the bananas?" Cindy, irrepressible as always, demanded.

"I have to make a four-tiered wedding cake." Nicole threw up her hands in a very Gallic gesture.

Cindy sobered at once. "Tough luck. I'll cross my fingers for you."

Nicole, who had never attempted anything quite so ambitious, grinned ruefully. "*Merci.* I need all the help I can get."

A few minutes later, her hands already covered with flour, Nicole was called to the phone by Mollie. Cindy, glancing over her shoulder, winced at Nicole's expression. As soon as the eldest Lewis hung up the receiver, she demanded, "All right, what happened at the picnic? Why did Mr. Whitney call to thank me for the ride in the antique Rolls? What antique Rolls?"

Cindy and Mollie looked at each other. "It's my fault," Mollie admitted. "We had this slight landslide, Nicole."

By the time they had explained, Nicole was so upset she inadvertently ran her floury hands through her brown hair. Looking as though the work was making her prematurely gray, she exclaimed, "Can't you two be trusted with the simplest task?"

"Stow it, Nicole," Cindy threatened, "or you'll be slicing bananas by yourself, and you'll be here till next Christmas. The man was pleased with his picnic, wasn't he? Who cares where we served it?"

"*Idiot!*" Nicole shouted. But the picnic was behind them, and right now she had the wedding cake to complete. The scolding her two sisters so richly deserved would have to wait.

The rest of the day passed uneventfully. The

number of banana-inspired desserts in the large refrigerator grew steadily, and Nicole, while her cake baked, whipped up some tasty salmon mousse and poured it into two fish-shaped molds.

"Those will look nice surrounded by crackers and parsley," she told herself out loud. "Mollie, do you know how to make melon balls?"

"No, but I'll be happy to learn." Mollié was fast becoming as tired of bananas as she had been of mushrooms the day before, and she was anxious to start working with a different kind of food.

"What about me?" Cindy griped.

"You've got whipped cream on your nose."

"Aside from that." Cindy went temporarily cross-eyed as she wiped off the stray bit of cream, then licked it off her finger. "Hmmm, good. What can I do now? And no more bananas, please!"

"You can start making canapés. How many are left, anyhow?"

"Canapés?"

"No, *idiot.* Bananas."

"I was afraid that was what you meant." Cindy grinned. "Too many. Any more auctions going on?"

Nicole shook her head. The sound of a shrill buzzer sent her flying toward the big ovens. "That's my cake."

By the time they left the shop, Nicole felt that preparations for the two big weekend events were well in hand. Except for the stacks of bananas, she assured herself, all was well. She crossed her fingers against any more bad luck.

Chapter 7

*O*n *Saturday morning, they reached the cater-*ing shop extra early, as Nicole experienced last-minute qualms about the wedding. Cindy, grumpy because she hadn't had time for her usual Saturday morning jog with her dad, followed her sisters into the shop, sighing as she smelled the rapidly overripening bananas.

"Nicole, we've got to do something about these bananas. The whole shop stinks!"

Nicole responded with unusual fierceness. "You think of something, then, smarty!"

"Okay, I will," Cindy snapped, and stalked off to start assembling canapés.

"What's wrong, Nicole?" Mollie asked her older sister timidly.

"Oh, I'm just nervous," Nicole admitted. "I've still got to get that wedding cake assembled."

"But you spent all afternoon yesterday decorating each layer. They're all wrapped and safely stored in the freezer."

"But I still have to put it all together," Nicole said. "*Mon dieu,* did I call the rental shop about the tables and chairs and the canopy for the wedding? Mom usually uses tons of assistants for a wedding, but since this one's being done on a tiny budget, she didn't hire anybody extra. I wonder if she realized how hard it would be. I don't see how we can possibly do all this work ourselves."

Mollie blanched, but Cindy, overhearing the frantic note in her sister's voice, relented enough to say, "Relax, Nicole. You called yesterday about the chairs. I heard you."

"All right, you go collect them and deliver them to the wedding site. We'll get everything set up first."

"What about the canapés?"

"Mollie can work on them. We have most of them already made, anyhow. And you two did a good job on the picnic the other day."

Mollie rolled her eyes at Cindy, who ignored her. "I'll be back in an hour," Cindy said.

She quickly unloaded the tables and other equipment on the small but well-groomed backyard where the wedding was scheduled to occur, then returned to the shop for the linen and other decorations. Just as she walked into the shop, Cindy heard a shriek.

"What's wrong?" she yelled, hurrying through the back door.

"My cake! It's in shambles!" Nicole sobbed, while Mollie stared wide-eyed at the second layer of the cake, lying in pieces atop the bottom layer.

"Gosh." Cindy gulped. "What happened?"

"I don't know, I was trying to be so careful." Nicole's face looked as pale as the delicate white cake itself. Cindy, more alarmed at the sight of her usually serene older sister's panic than she was by the sight of the crumbled pastry, tried to think.

She inspected the cake more closely. "Doesn't Mom put a circle of cardboard under each layer to support it before she puts it on the little columns?"

"Quel idiot!"

"Hey, all I said was—" Cindy began.

"I meant me," Nicole explained. "How could I have been so stupid?"

"Because you're a bundle of nerves," Cindy told her frankly. "Calm down, Nicole. Everything's going to be all right."

"But the cake," the eldest Lewis sister wailed. "No one can have a wedding without a cake!"

"Look, all that's ruined is one layer; the bottom one is okay. Just take off the pieces and smooth out the icing a little. Can't you bake another layer quickly? The wedding doesn't start until two o'clock."

"I guess I'll have to," Nicole decided, trying to pull her scattered thoughts together. "Is everything set up?"

"I set up the tables and chairs, but I forgot the tablecloths, and I haven't put up the canopy. Why'd they want a canopy, anyhow? It's a beautiful day."

"They didn't want to take any chances," Nicole told her with a sigh. "Good thing they can't see their cake right now!" She managed a small smile. "Okay, you two take the rest of the food, finish the tables, and lay out the buffet. Then leave Mollie to keep an eye on the table, and you come back for me and the cake. With any luck, I should have it ready on time."

With Mollie's help, Cindy loaded the station wagon, and they set out. When they reached the client's house and turned into a narrow drive, Mollie looked around. "Wow, Cin, look at those roses," she said, admiring the bushes in full bloom.

"We don't have time to admire the scenery," Cindy said as she parked the station wagon carefully. "Help me get this stuff out, Mollie."

Mollie, who had been thinking of romantic walks alongside rose bushes, snickered but helped her sister to unload the station wagon. They both had their hands full when a stout woman in pale pink suddenly appeared behind them.

"Who are you? Where's Mrs. Lewis?"

Mollie, startled, looking instinctively at Cindy,

who said, "We're Mrs. Lewis's daughters; we're helping out today."

"But where's Mrs. Lewis?"

Cindy squared her shoulders and prepared for the worst. "Mom's in the hospital; she had emergency surgery a few days ago."

"Oh no!" the woman moaned. "First Sarah got her train stuck in the door and ripped it, now this!"

"Everything's going to be fine, honest," Cindy tried to reassure their alarmed client.

"I knew I should have hired a bigger catering company." Mrs. Danus wrung her hands together. "But this isn't a very big wedding, and Mrs. Lewis came so highly recommended! I also thought I might save some money using Movable Feasts. I should have known something would go wrong. Oh, dear, oh, dear."

Cindy bristled, but before she could protest, a small child, dressed in pink organdy, ran up behind them, crying, "Mama, come quick, Sarah's locked herelf in her bedroom. She says she's not coming down with a tear in her train." The mother of the bride threw up her hands, moaning, and she and the little girl both hurried off. Cindy grinned, and the sisters returned to their job.

After the tablecloths were laid out, the florist arrived with the flowers, and Mollie was happy to chat with the two young deliverymen while the elaborate floral displays were set up.

"Mollie," Cindy called, "come over here and help me!"

Mollie reluctantly said good-bye to the cute blond assistant and went back to her sister's side.

"Aren't we almost done?"

"Are you kidding? There's more food to put out, then I've got to get back and pick up Nicole and the cake. She'll want to inspect the buffet table before the crowd arrives. Then—oh, my gosh."

"What?"

"I forgot to set up the canopy. Come help me."

Cindy needed all her strength to push the poles into the hard-packed ground. Then together they stretched out the canvas, and Cindy pulled the first corner taut, showing Mollie how to tie a square knot.

"Like this, see? Got it?"

"I know how to tie a knot," Mollie answered. "Don't treat me like such an idiot. I took a macrame class, remember?"

"Okay. You take care of this, then. I'll take a look when I get back."

Mollie, watching her sister hurry away, quickly tied two loose knots and turned her attention back to the cute blond arranging the flowers.

When Cindy reached the catering shop, she found Nicole waiting impatiently.

"What took you so long? Do you know what time it is?"

"Relax," Cindy soothed. "We're doing fine."

"Say that *after* we get the cake there in one piece," Nicole told her.

Cindy looked at the large cake, then at her sister. "Nicole, it looks great. You did a terrific job."

Nicole relaxed slightly at the sincerity in her sister's tone. "Thanks. You really think it looks good?"

"Professional as they come," Cindy promised. "Now let's get it into the back of the wagon."

With the utmost care, the cake was positioned in the rear of the automobile, on top of a clean cloth.

"I think I should drive," Nicole began, but Cindy shook her head.

"Not while you're still as nervous as a cat in a dog kennel! I'll do it."

"Drive carefully," Nicole begged, and they set off.

They reached the first intersection without mishap, and Nicole, who had twisted to keep an eye on the precious cake, was almost beginning to think their problems were over when a sudden gasp from her sister made her turn.

She was just in time to see a dilapidated truck careen madly through a red light, brake belatedly, and slide, screeching, into the front of their wagon.

"Oh no!" Nicole shrieked as they rocked under the impact.

Cindy, more alarmed than she would have admitted, clung to the steering wheel so that no one could see how her hands were shaking. "What kind of shape is our car in?" she murmured, afraid to see the damage. "That man must be crazy."

"*Oh, là là,* forget about the car. What about the cake?" Nicole gasped.

They both jumped out. Cindy, opening the car door, thought for a moment that the California skies had released a freak snowstorm. Then she realized that it was feathers floating in the air, and the ungodly noise she heard came from the back of the old truck, where dozens of disturbed chickens squawked in protest.

"Just didn't see the light, I reckon," the man with the grizzled beard was saying, shaking his head at the damage to his truck. "Must be getting old."

Cindy bit back a fervent agreement and inspected their car. Fortunately, the damage was minor. She found a sharp dent in the fender, but otherwise the station wagon appeared unharmed.

"We should notify the police," she told the old man, who continued to shake his head and mutter to himself. They had collected several spectators, including a sturdy young man from the gas station on the corner who asked, "Want me to call for you?"

"Please." Cindy nodded. She left the truck driver to his soliloquy and turned back to Nicole. "That guy's a little nuts," she told her sister. "How's the cake?"

"I'm afraid to look," Nicole muttered. Sure enough, both hands covered her face as her body shuddered with nervous spasms.

"Nicole, take it easy." Cindy sounded worried as she tried to calm her older sister.

"I can't bake another cake. There isn't time. What are we going to do? The wedding will be ruined!"

"Let's take a look before you start having fits," Cindy urged. She pulled her sister to the back of the station wagon, and very cautiously they opened the rear panel.

"I knew it—it's ruined!" Nicole shrieked.

"Hold on." Cindy grabbed her sister's arm. "The top layer just slid off, it's not even broken."

"Do you think I can put it back on without it falling apart?" Nicole asked.

"Sure you can," Cindy assured her, crossing her fingers behind her back and hardly daring to breathe as Nicole attempted the delicate process.

"I did it!" The two girls hugged each other.

"Let's go."

"We have to wait for the police," Cindy told her sister.

"We don't have time." Nicole groaned. "We're going to be late!"

"We have to, Nicole. It's the law."

Nicole looked as if she was about to cry. "Did you tell them it's an emergency? We have a tardy cake on our hands."

Cindy, not sure that the Santa Barbara police

would consider that a bona fide emergency, didn't answer. Nicole began to pace up and down beside the station wagon.

"Aren't they ever coming?"

By the time a patrol car appeared and an officer inspected the vehicles and took down all the pertinent details, Nicole was muttering angrily under her breath, glancing continually at her watch. At last they were able to go, and Cindy, praying hard for no more accidents, backed their car carefully away from the battered old truck.

"Do you think this accident will affect my driving record, Nicole?" Cindy asked worriedly.

Nicole, pulling her thoughts away from the wedding, tried to focus on her sister's anxious tone. "I don't think so. It wasn't your fault, Cindy. We were sitting still, waiting for the light to change, for goodness' sake. We'll ask Dad."

Her thoughts returned to more urgent matters. "If we're just on time! Hurry, Cindy."

"I don't want to have another accident," Cindy pointed out.

"I know!" Nicole agreed. "But drive as fast as the speed limit allows!"

When they reached the house, Cindy had hardly parked the car when Nicole jumped out, urging, "Come help me with the cake! Thank heavens the ceremony hasn't started yet!"

"Maybe the bride's still locked in her bedroom," Cindy murmured.

"What?" Nicole flashed her an inquiring gaze.

"Nothing."

When they had safely carried the heavy cake to the correct table, Nicole hurried off to inspect the rest of the buffet. Cindy made a private vow that if she were ever crazy enough to marry, she would definitely elope. All this fuss—good grief!

An elderly lady approached the table and leaned closer to peer through her glasses. "Decorating with feathers—how unusual."

Cindy, her face flushing, nodded mutely. When the guest continued past the table to take her seat in one of the chairs on the lawn, Cindy took a clean fork and began to defeather the cake, thankful that the bride's mother wasn't nearby.

"Isn't this romantic?" a familiar voice said from beside her. "They're almost ready to start, Cindy. What do we do now?"

"Stay out of the way, I guess," Cindy told her younger sister. "After the ceremony, Nicole will cut the cake, and you and I get to hand out champagne. Carefully!"

Mollie looked indignant. "You needn't imply that I can't pass a tray without spilling something." She turned as the organ that had been quietly playing paused and struck up a new tune. "Listen, they're about to start the wedding march."

While Mollie stood on tiptoe, straining to catch the first glimpse of the bride, Cindy turned to look at the minister and the groom, who, along with his two ushers, had taken his place beneath the canopy. The canopy swayed slightly in the breeze—

Wait a minute, Cindy thought, suddenly alert. There isn't any breeze.

As she watched, frozen in horror, one end of the canopy began to sag, and the men beneath it looked up in alarm.

"Oh no." Cindy moaned. "Mollie, run and tell the organist to stall—play it again, anything."

"Me? Do I have to?" Mollie sputtered.

"Either that or watch the groom suffocate under our canopy," Cindy warned. Mollie ran off, while Cindy hurried to the canopy.

"What the—" one of the men was saying.

"It's all right, sir. One of the knots has slipped. I'll just tighten the line."

Cindy, red-faced, could hear a quiet murmur of laughter from the guests as she quickly secured the heavy canvas, then checked the other lines to prevent any more accidents.

"Okay." She waved to the watching organist, and for the second time the familiar notes of the wedding march flowed smoothly from the musician's skilled fingers.

Cindy rejoined her sisters behind the buffet table, where Nicole, a fixed smile on her face, muttered under her breath, "How embarrassing! Cindy, how could you?"

"It wasn't me, I know how to tie a knot!" Cindy's quick temper flared. "Mollie was the one who goofed—again!"

"Mollie—" Nicole began, through gritted teeth.

But the youngest Lewis was deaf to reprimands. "Just *look* at that wedding gown," she whispered happily. "Isn't the bride lovely! Did you say something, Nicole?"

Nicole groaned.

Chapter 8

*B*y the time the bride and groom departed in a flurry of rice, Nicole's whole body ached with fatigue. "I never knew Mother had such a hard job," she murmured to Cindy, who was fidgeting impatiently, waiting to start to clean up.

"She doesn't get as bent out of shape as you do," Cindy pointed out. "Of course, she probably doesn't have to contend with chicken farmers who don't know how to drive, either." Cindy grinned. Now that the accident was over, the whole thing had become rather funny. On the other hand, she remembered, she hadn't yet informed her dad about the car. Her smile faded.

"Can we start putting away the food now?" she demanded, anxious to get home and get the ordeal over with.

"I guess so." Nicole looked around the spacious lawn. "Most of the guests are leaving." She began to collect the half-empty plates and sticky wineglasses, packing them carefully to avoid breakage.

Cindy, working alongside her, asked, her voice anxious, "You don't think Dad will take away my driving privileges, do you, Nicole?"

"It wasn't your fault, Cindy," Nicole repeated for the hundredth time. "Stop worrying."

"Easier said than done." Cindy sighed. "Where's Mollie?"

"One guess," Nicole told her.

Cindy looked around for the nearest good-looking guy. Sure enough, a young man of medium height, hands thrust into his linen jacket, lounged beside the canopy, deep in conversation with their delighted little sister.

"Good grief," Cindy muttered aloud. "Mollie!"

Her shout made several people stare, and Nicole flushed. "Cindy, *mon dieu*. A little more tact, *s'il te plaît*."

"She can help clean up," Cindy argued. "This is no time for flirting with the customers. I've got a date with Grant tonight!"

Mollie, her eyes still sparkling from the stranger's attentions, hurried over.

"What is it?"

"Get to work, shrimp. We want to get out of here."

"Oh, all right," Mollie said, with one last wave

at the young man under the canopy. "But Alex is such a total hunk, Cindy. And he was so sweet about the champagne."

"Champagne?" Nicole, suddenly alert, looked up accusingly at her little sister. "Did you spill—"

"Only one glass," Mollie hastened to reassure her. "And he was *so* nice about it, he's positive the stain will come out."

Nicole groaned.

Mollie, oblivious, continued to chatter. "And he has the dreamiest blue eyes, Nicole. He's the best-looking boy I've met in at least—"

"Two days," Cindy finished dryly. "Here, shrimp. Take this tray and collect dirty glasses. And don't spill anything else!"

Mollie, too elated to be disturbed by her sister's warning, took the tray and floated away.

"I'll take down the canopy and start folding up the chairs; we're going to have to make more than one trip to collect all the furniture," Cindy observed.

"All right," Nicole said. "I'll keep working on the glassware."

It seemed forever before the cleanup was completed, the furniture and extra glassware returned to the rental supply house, and their own utensils taken back to the shop. They locked up and started home, Cindy worrying continually about being late for her date and having to face her dad.

They were surprised to find all the animals in

the garage when they got there. Winston, their friendly Newfoundland, woofed happily as they parked the car. Mollie paused to give the big black dog a hug, and Nicole patted Smokey and Cinders as the cats rubbed against her ankles. Cindy, who for once had no time to spare for her beloved animals, rushed on through the kitchen door.

As soon as she stepped over the threshold at a fast run, her feet slipped out from under her and she hit the floor with a thump, sliding halfway across the spacious kitchen.

"Ugh," she grunted, rubbing her now-damp posterior. She heard her dad call from the den.

"Don't let the animals in; the floor is wet."

"Now he tells me," Cindy commented, turning to yell at the other girls. But it was too late; Winston galloped across the clean floor, leaving a trail of large paw prints behind him, anxious to inspect the body sprawled across the smooth tile.

"I'm fine, boy," Cindy told him, pushing his damp muzzle away. "But you're making a mess."

Nicole paused at the doorway. "The floor's wet, Mollie; better go around."

They did, while Cindy stood up, rubbing her sore bottom. She pushed Winston gently back outside and mopped up the marks on the floor.

"Who mopped the floor?" Mollie, who had come in through the patio door, asked from the hall.

"I did," Richard Lewis told them, grinning over

Mollie's shoulder. "Although Cindy seems to be applying the finishing touches."

Cindy turned back. "I didn't notice in time," she explained. She hung the mop back in the pantry and turned to face her father, trying to sound casual. "Dad, we had this little accident today—"

Richard Lewis regarded her sternly. "How bad? Anyone hurt?"

"Oh no," Nicole assured him.

"It's only a dent in the fender. Not a *big* dent," Cindy said.

"And it wasn't Cindy's fault. We were sitting at a stoplight—" Nicole began.

"Don't be mad at Cindy," Mollie urged at the same time.

"Hold on, hold on. One at a time," Mr. Lewis ordered. When he had heard all the details and inspected the battered fender, he came back inside, where the girls waited anxiously.

"You won't take away my driving privileges, will you, Dad?" Cindy asked, watching his expression for a clue.

"She didn't mean to—" Mollie added.

"It wouldn't be fair—"

"Hold it!" Mr. Lewis thundered. "Don't start all over again. I didn't say a word about punishing Cindy. She doesn't seem to be at fault, so I'm not going to throw her to the lions. Not yet, anyhow."

Cindy breathed a sigh of relief, giving him a brief hug before she glanced at her watch. "Oh, gosh, I've got to get ready!" She disappeared through the doorway, heading for the shower and a quick change.

"I could have mopped the floor tonight." Nicole, looking at the neat kitchen, sounded guilty.

Mr. Lewis shook his head. "No reason for you girls to do all the work. I noticed the floor seemed rather sticky—"

"I spilled some juice last night," Mollie confessed, looking sheepish. "But I thought I got it all up, honest."

"And I've got some hamburgers ready to grill out back," Mr. Lewis continued. "Then we'll go down and visit your mother."

"Great," Nicole said, relieved that she had no more work to do tonight.

"Oh, and the modeling agency called, Nicole. Your agent was delighted to hear that you didn't make that trip to the East Coast after all. One of his other models has the flu, and he needs someone to take her place at the big fashion-show brunch tomorrow morning."

"Oh, I can't." Nicole looked distressed. "We have another reception to cater tomorrow, and—"

Richard Lewis frowned. "Nicole, I think you're letting this job get out of hand. Your mother appreciates your efforts, but we don't want you to give up all your own activities."

"But, Dad," Nicole began. The sudden shrill of the telephone sent Mollie running to pick up the receiver. "It's for you, Dad."

"I'll be back in a minute," Mr. Lewis promised,

then headed for his study, in case it was a business call.

"Saved by the bell." Mollie frowned at her sister. "What's the matter with you, Nicole?"

"I don't know what you mean." Nicole sounded defensive as she brushed her brown hair back from her eyes, almost too tired to lift her hand.

"You've either got to tell Dad the truth or stop making such a production. He'll be suspicious if you can't leave the catering shop for a moment."

"But what about the reception tomorrow afternoon?" Nicole, feeling an absurd desire to sit down and cry, shut her eyes to block out her sister's frown.

"That's not until three, and we've got most of the food already prepared. There's no wedding cake to make this time, thank heavens. Relax, Nicole. I don't know why you're making such a big deal out of this."

"I just want everything to be perfect."

"We got through today all right, didn't we?"

Nicole shuddered, thinking of all the near disasters that had been so narrowly averted. "By the skin of our teeth!"

"We'll manage tomorrow, too. And if something goes wrong, at least we gave it our best try."

But Nicole still seemed troubled. "I wanted to prove that I could handle everything," she murmured, so low that Mollie wasn't quite sure what she said.

"What?" the other girl asked.

"I'm not a kid anymore," Nicole said. "A good try isn't enough."

"I don't get it," Mollie said.

"It's just—" Nicole began, when the doorbell suddenly chimed and Mollie jumped.

"That must be Grant; I'll tell Cindy." She hurried up the stairs, and Nicole called after her, "I'll let him in."

The moment was gone, and Nicole, who hardly understood herself just why it was so important that she make the catering shop successful in her mother's absence, sighed as she went to open the door. She met her dad in the hallway, intent upon the same errand.

"Of course I'll model tomorrow," she told him, and Richard Lewis smiled.

"That's good; I knew you wouldn't let them down. Alain offered the whole family tickets. I'm sorry your mother will have to miss it," Mr. Lewis said as he opened the front door. "Hello, Grant," he greeted the tall, dark-haired young man waiting patiently on the doorstep

"Hi, Mr. Lewis, Nicole." Grant nodded to them both. "Is Cindy ready?"

Upstairs, Cindy hastily pulled on her denim skirt and a new aqua blouse, then ran a brush through her still-damp hair. She had already started toward the stairs when Mollie grabbed her.

"Wait a minute, is that all you're going to do? I

thought you said you wanted to look really nice tonight."

"I did." Cindy sounded defensive. "I had to give up all our surfing together this week, and Grant's been so nice about it—"

She bit her lip. Grant had been part of her life since almost the first week of school. She did want to please him, but dressing up was more in Mollie's line. The hoydenish middle Lewis felt comfortable only in jeans. She looked at herself uncertainly in the mirror. "I did put on the new blouse Nicole said I should buy."

"It's gorgeous," Mollie approved. "But you need a little makeup, Cindy. Let me do it."

Cindy sat down reluctantly while Mollie whipped out what seemed to be a small mountain of cosmetics. "Just a little eye shadow and some eye liner—don't blink!"

"I'm trying," Cindy grumbled. "But you poked that brush in my eye!"

"Don't be such a baby. You can stand a little makeup," Mollie said sternly. "Now hold still."

When Cindy bounded down the steps, released at last from Mollie's tutelage, the expertly applied makeup combined with the new aqua blouse made her green eyes seem as clear and brilliant as a tropical ocean. Grant, his familiar lopsided grin wavering, stood and stared for a moment, his greeting forgotten. Cindy didn't even notice.

"Bye, Dad," she called. "We'll swing by and see

Mom for a minute, then we're meeting the gang at Golf'n'Stuff."

Mollie hung over the stairwell, watching her sister go, a disgusted expression on her face. "I coaxed her into using some makeup, and it looks like Grant loved it. That big dummy didn't even notice the impression she made on him!"

Mr. Lewis chuckled. "That's Cindy; she's probably thinking about beating everyone at miniature golf tonight."

He started for the patio to put on the hamburgers, and Mollie followed, chattering about the importance of wearing exactly the right shade of eye makeup. Nicole watched them go. The other two girls didn't seem overwhelmed by their new responsibilities. Why did it matter so much to her? "They're just kids," she murmured stubbornly to herself. "It's different for me."

When you were almost eighteen, failing at an adult task seemed intolerable. It was a natural feeling, Nicole assured herself as she slowly climbed the stairs. Wasn't it?

Chapter 9

*O*n Sunday morning Nicole managed to put aside her worries about the catering shop long enough to give her usual poised performance in the fashion show. Richard Lewis, who had never before had the opportunity to see his daughter at work, watched proudly as she strolled up and down the platform. Nicole modeled one fashionable outfit after another, looking very calm and quite lovely, and her father found that he had to swallow rather hard.

After the show, Nicole tried to hurry, but first she had to dress and remove the heavy makeup demanded by the bright lights. Then Alain appeared to thank her for filling in at the last minute. By the time Nicole met her father outside the auditorium, she was alarmed to see Cindy and Mollie were missing.

"Where are the girls?" she asked her father.

"Cindy was in a rush to get to the beach; she's afraid it might rain later. She and Mollie took a bus home."

Nicole, aghast at this gross dereliction of duty, barely bit back a scathing denunciation. Those little brats, Nicole thought to herself. They know we have that reception this afternoon!

When they finally got home, it didn't help to discover that Cindy had taken the station wagon. Still fuming, Nicole shared a quick lunch with her dad, then took a bus down to the shop.

"I'm going to murder her with my bare hands," she promised herself aloud, causing an elderly woman seated beside her on the bus to stare in alarm, then move quietly to another seat.

Nicole sighed. When she reached her stop, she walked beneath overcast skies half a block to the catering shop, dug in her purse for the key, and discovered that it was missing.

Now what?

"Mon dieu," Nicole murmured. "Where could the key have gone?"

A sudden sound made her turn, and the station wagon, with Cindy behind the wheel and Mollie beside her, pulled into the back parking lot.

"Weren't the waves high enough?"

Cindy grinned, ignoring the sarcasm in her sister's question. " 'Bout time you showed up."

"What?" Nicole frowned, her bewilderment obvious. "Didn't you go to the beach? You told Dad—"

"That was just an excuse to leave early; I knew you'd be tied up after the show, and I had an idea."

"What have you been up to?" Nicole demanded, not quite trusting the smug smile on Cindy's face as she and Mollie exchanged conspiratorial glances.

"You'll see." Cindy took the purloined key from her jeans pocket and unlocked the back door to the shop.

Nicole walked through the doorway, looking about suspiciously. For a moment she saw nothing different about the kitchen, then a sense of something lacking made her pause. All at once Nicole realized what was missing—the heavy smell of overripe bananas.

"The bananas!" Nicole hurried to the front room. Sure enough, the crates of fruit were gone.

"What did you do—throw them out?"

Cindy looked offended. "Of course not, not after we paid for them. I donated the fruit to the Santa Barbara Zoo. Monkeys love very ripe bananas, so I hear."

Cindy grinned widely as Nicole broke into startled laughter. "And it's also tax deductible," she assured her older sister.

Nicole, wiping away tears of laughter, hugged her sister. "Cindy, that was inspired. And thank heavens we're rid of those bananas!"

Mollie, pleased to see Nicole restored to good spirits, added, "I helped move the crates, Nicole."

"Good for you," Nicole said with approval. A glance at her watch sobered her quickly. "We'd better get busy. Let's get all the food assembled for the Arts Committee reception."

Cindy, wickedly humming "Yes, We Have No Bananas," followed her sister into the kitchen.

Nicole, with one more load off her mind, felt more optimistic than she had since they started this mad venture. Maybe today there would be no disasters!

Working together, they loaded the station wagon and drove to the art gallery where the reception was to be held. A stout woman in a lavender dress greeted them. "Are you from Movable Feasts? Where's Mrs. Lewis?"

"That's our mother," Nicole explained. "She had to have emergency surgery last week, Mrs. . . . ?"

"Mrs. Field. I'm vice-president in charge of social activities. Oh, dear, oh, dear, what about our reception?"

"Don't worry, Mrs. Field," Nicole said firmly. "We have everything under control. If you'll just show us where to set up the buffet table, we can get started."

"Of course." The woman fluttered her hands in a nervous gesture that made Nicole wish for extra patience. "I think we're going to be in the director's room, no, or was that—"

The girls waited impatiently. Cindy, who was

holding a heavy hamper of food, began to mutter under her breath, drawing a quick look of censure from her older sister. Mrs. Field called to a tall young man who was standing with his back to her.

"Rob! Where do we want the food set up?"

"In the large meeting room, Mrs. Field. We agreed on it yesterday," the young man answered calmly. He walked toward them and directed a friendly smile toward all three girls.

Nicole, attracted by his good-natured expression, smiled back. "If you'll just show us the way—"

"Certainly. Can I give you a hand?"

Cindy shook her head. "I'm fine."

With a quiet efficiency that came as a welcome relief after the vice-president's dithering, he ushered them into a long room, pointed out two tables set up for their use, then introduced himself.

"I'm Rob O'Neal. I work here part-time as sort of an all-around gofer when I'm not in class at UCSB."

"Really?" Nicole, intrigued by the humor in his intelligent hazel eyes, felt a rush of instantaneous pleasure that she hadn't experienced in months. Steady, *idiot,* she told herself silently. You're too old to have a crush.

Whether she was too old or not, the tall young man with his broad shoulders and dark wavy hair certainly made her pulse quicken. And she noticed, holding back a frown, that he'd made an impression on Mollie, too. She was gazing up at him with wide eyes.

"Mollie," she said, more sharply than she intended, "go back and get the tablecloths, please."

Mollie blinked at her sister in surprise. "You're holding them," she pointed out.

"Oh, of course," Nicole murmured, feeling incredibly foolish.

But Rob didn't seem to notice. He was helping Cindy lift the heavy hamper onto the table with such easy charm that she didn't even bristle.

Nicole hurried to lay out the white linen, then put Mollie to work unloading the food. She picked up a large jug and turned to Rob.

"Can you show me where to get some water to mix the punch?"

"Sure." He led the way to a water cooler, and Nicole, her usual poise a little shaky, asked shyly, "What are you studying?"

Rob smiled at her. "Don't laugh. I'm majoring in art history."

"Mais non!" Nicole hurried to assure him. "I wouldn't laugh. I think that's marvelous. I'm interested in art history myself. Why should I laugh?"

"Some of my friends don't think the subject macho enough," Rob said with a grin.

Nicole, covertly inspecting his broad shoulders and firm, athletic build, thought to herself that *macho* was an immensely inadequate term to apply to such an intelligent, personable guy.

"Careful," Rob said, his hazel eyes twinkling.

With a start, Nicole realized that her jug was about to overflow. She gave herself a mental shake even as she smiled up at the young man.

"Thanks. I'd better get the punch made."

"If I can do anything else, just yell," Rob offered, adding, "I hope you can spare some time away from the buffet. There are some nice paintings here, aside from the special sculpture exhibit. It would be a shame to miss them while you're here. I'll show you my favorites."

"I'd like that." Nicole's smile deepened, and the glow in her soft blue eyes made Rob linger another moment. "After the reception, I'll reserve some time for us to look around."

"Terrific," Rob assured her before turning back to his other duties.

Nicole, sighing happily to herself, tried to decide if it was merely their common interest in art that made her feel like dancing around the room. She suspected not.

Humming a French folk song beneath her breath, she hurried back to the tables. Cindy and Mollie had spread out the canapés and were lining up fruit trays and small desserts.

"Good job," Nicole said. "Help me get out the big punch bowls, Cindy."

Cindy, wondering what had brought about this change in mood, helped Nicole lift the heavy silver bowls from their box and unwrap the white paper that protected them. Then Nicole carefully mixed a champagne punch and another nonalcoholic fruit punch, adding ice cubes from an insulated cooler and floating a few slices of oranges and lemons on top.

"Very pretty," Cindy said. Nicole smiled happily.

"I'm going to the car to make sure we didn't forget anything," she announced.

Cindy, watching her older sister waltz out of the room, wondered aloud, "What happened to her?"

Mollie snorted. "Don't be dense, Cindy. Didn't you see that totally gorgeous guy? Wish he'd look at me the way he stares at Nicole!"

"He's too old for you," Cindy said automatically, but she whistled quietly to herself. The truth was, Rob O'Neal had impressed her, too, and Nicole hadn't had a special guy in quite a while. That should keep her from grumbling, Cindy decided, pleased at the thought. It would be nice to have something to keep her in a good mood for a change.

Nicole returned with an extra jar of nuts, checked the tables one more time, then stationed Mollie at one end with the plates, while she and Cindy began to ladle punch into small cups.

Mollie, aware that she had been placed as far from the liquid refreshment as possible, squirmed in boredom. She really had nothing to do except smile sweetly as the art patrons began to file through the reception area. While the minutes passed slowly, she allowed her eyes to wander over the crowd, stopping when she spotted a pair of familiar-looking shoulders. Could it really be him?

"Nicole." She hissed at her sister. "Can I go look around for a while? You don't need me here."

"What for?"

"I want to look at the artwork," Mollie said, her blue eyes innocent.

Nicole frowned. Mollie interested in art? Still, how could she discourage any hint of genuine cultural curiosity? "All right," she agreed. "But stay out of trouble."

"Who, me?" Mollie widened her eyes, then giggled as Nicole threatened to throw a peanut her way. "Of course."

She wound her way through the crowded gallery, purposely following the path of the young man in the gray jacket. When he paused to compare two sculptures, Mollie managed to gently bump his arm.

"Oh, sorry—Alex!" she exclaimed, sounding just as surprised and delighted as if she hadn't tracked him through two rooms filled with sculptures.

"Hello, sweet Mollie." The young man's smile was particularly engaging, and his blue eyes dazzled her. "Don't tell me you're hard at work again?"

"Hardly working." Mollie made her threadbare joke sound almost fresh as she gazed at him with round eyes, openly admiring his handsome face. "My sister gave me some time off to look at the artwork."

"What do you think of the sculpture?"

Mollie turned to stare at the exhibit before them, trying to look appreciative, though she privately thought the contraption looked like a cross between a giant eggbeater and a slightly tipsy stack of jar lids. "Very interesting."

"Yes, he's quite experimental," Alex agreed solemnly. "Looks like it belongs in a junkyard, doesn't it?"

Mollie giggled, happy to abandon her role as an art lover. "You're telling me! Does he really sell these things?"

"For incredible prices," Alex assured her. "My father bought three as an investment. He says the uglier it is, nowadays, the more the art critics admire it."

They laughed together, while Mollie admired Alex's silver-gray jacket and open-necked cotton shirt. The pale tones set off his dark good looks admirably, and Mollie could feel her heart beating faster.

"There's the great artist himself," Alex was saying, and Mollie tore her gaze away from the young man's good-looking face to survey the crowd. She examined a stout man in a slightly damp brown suit. "That one?"

"No." Alex grinned. "That's a stockbroker, Mollie. The man with the beard."

"Good heavens," Mollie murmured. Most of the men in the room wore suits and ties. A few, like Alex, were dressed more casually but still neatly. The man with the straggly beard, however, wore a grimy T-shirt and faded jeans. "He looks like the janitor."

"Artists are supposed to be eccentric," Alex told her solemnly.

Mollie, not sure if he was joking again or not, simply nodded. "What sort of art do you admire?" she asked.

"I have some nice etchings at home; you should come up and see them sometime," Alex said, his tone playful.

Mollie, too innocent to recognize the ancient cliché, looked genuinely pleased. "Really? When?"

Alex laughed. Mollie bit back her smile, afraid that she'd said something wrong. "What did I say?"

"Nothing." Alex continued to chuckle. "You're a delight, Mollie. I haven't met anyone like you in ages. And I really would like to show you my home. I'm having some friends over Monday night, nothing elaborate. Would you like to come?"

A date with this incredibly handsome, sophisticated young man? Mollie's heart beat so fast that she was afraid he'd see her tremble. "That would be nice," she said cautiously, afraid to set off his inexplicable mirth once more. But Alex only smiled.

Meanwhile, the crowd at the refreshment table had thinned, and Nicole anxiously awaited the time when she could slip away for a few minutes with Rob.

"It would be a shame to stay here all afternoon

and not get to see the exhibit," she explained to Cindy.

"Uh-huh." Cindy nodded. "I saw the way you looked at that guy, and, more to the point, the way he looked at you. Don't tell me any fairy tales, Nicole!"

Nicole blushed. "He seems awfully nice, *n'est-ce pas?*"

"Sure," Cindy agreed. There was a time when she would have scoffed, but her own special feeling for Grant had given her new insight. Cindy no longer found it impossible to imagine the exhilarating rush of delight that came when you suspected that you'd met someone really special. "Go for it, kid."

Nicole smiled back at her sister, happier than she had been all week.

"Girls." The slightly complaining tone of Mrs. Field interrupted this pleasant moment of camaraderie, and Nicole grimaced. Count on the busy little woman to ruin all her plans. What did she want now?

"It's started to rain outside, and we have some latecomers," Mrs. Field told them, clucking anxiously at the thought. "One of you should collect their coats and put them away. Aside from common courtesy, we don't want them dripping on the exhibits. Mr. Laciel is very temperamental!"

"Cindy." Nicole threw her sister a silent appeal. "Will you take care of that, please?" She could see Rob waiting hopefully at the side of the room, and she had no desire to collect wet raincoats.

'What does the woman think I am? Some kind of porter?" Cindy mumbled under her breath, but she hurried to the entrance of the art gallery and accepted the guests' coats and umbrellas.

One matron with perfectly groomed gray hair handed over her mink jacket rather reluctantly. "You will keep an eye on my mink, won't you, dear?"

Cindy, trying to look dependable, hastened to reassure her. "Absolutely."

When the spate of latercomers seemed to have subsided, Cindy felt it safe to leave, but what was she to do with her armload of damp garments?

She looked through the front of the gallery for a cloakroom without success. One door led to a tiny bathroom, with no place to hang clothes; another was an office that looked very official, and damp coats wouldn't do much for the paperwork atop the director's desk. Finally Cindy located another small room that was empty except for one large, rather crooked clothes rack of metal and wood.

"This should do it," Cindy said out loud to herself. She hung up the coats and umbrellas, taking extra care with the mink jacket. One worry was resolved, but another came quickly to her mind. Cindy, suddenly uncertain whether she'd brought in all the trays of canapés that Nicole had packed, looked around. How was she supposed to be in two places at once, for Pete's sake? Finally she spotted Mollie, making cow's eyes at a good-looking young man.

"Mollie!" She hissed.

Mollie reluctantly looked around. What do you want?"

"Come here and watch the coats for me; I need to go back outside."

"Sure." Mollie nodded. As Cindy hurried away, Mollie turned back to her new friend, without even a glance at the small room.

Meanwhile Nicole, wandering happily through the gallery by the side of the tall young assistant, barely noticed the sculptures. She and Rob seemed to have so many interests in common. Though not as dedicated a fan of French culture as Nicole, Rob was quite knowledgeable about her favorite area of art, and they talked on and on. Nicole, happily absorbed in comparing modern European painters, almost forgot her earlier delight in Rob's broad shoulders and warm hazel eyes.

So intent were the two upon their own conversation that it was a moment before either noticed that a sudden hush had fallen over the room. Nicole looked inquiringly at Rob when she realized that the noisy chatter had stilled.

"Time for the unveiling of Laciel's most important new creation."

"How exciting."

Rob grinned. "Wait till you see the sculpture

before you comment. I caught a glimpse of it earlier; he wouldn't put it out with the rest—said it deserved a room to itself."

With Rob's tall form cutting tactfully through the crowd, Nicole found herself led to the front, where she could get a good view of the great event. She didn't see Cindy, but Mollie was visible toward the back, talking animatedly to a very good-looking young man, not paying the least bit of attention to the art. After mentally scolding her youngest, uncultured sister, Nicole turned her attention back to Mrs. Field, who had just introduced the artist.

"Today you see my greatest creation," the bearded man announced. "This is a day that will long be remembered!"

With a flourish he threw open the door, and the crowd stretched to peer into the small room.

"Aiee!" the artist screamed. "My art—what have they done?"

With a terrible sense of foreboding, Nicole saw a haphazard structure of steel and wood, almost hidden beneath a collection of damp coats and dripping umbrellas. "Oh, no," she whispered, too chagrined to speak as the scrawny artist ran toward his maligned sculpture, anxious to remove the offending garments.

Meanwhile, Cindy, hurrying back into the gallery, suddenly saw a grungy-looking vagrant grabbing at the mink jacket.

"Hey," she yelled. "That's not yours!"

With a sudden spurt of speed well known to Vista High's water polo team, Cindy threw herself at the thief, knocking him flat upon the hardwood floor, just short of the clothes pole. Together they slid toward the sculpture, which shook alarmingly, but just managed to stay upright. But one large black umbrella, dislodged by the sudden jolt, fell, hitting the already-bemused artist just behind the neck.

He sank weakly back to the floor. "It is a conspiracy, yes?" he murmured to Cindy. "You are from *Art Today*; they didn't like my last showing, either."

Then, while the onlookers shrieked, he sank back into a semifaint. Cindy stared at him, bewildered.

Nicole, groaning, hid her face in the folds of Rob's coat.

Chapter 10

*O*n Monday morning, Nicole's alarm awakened her rudely. Groaning, she groped for the button to shut off the irritating whine. A second, softer noise followed, like an echo, and Nicole pried open one eye to see Cinders sitting beside the bed, purring sweetly.

"How can you be in such a good mood so early in the morning?" Nicole demanded sleepily.

The young cat changed his tune and began to yowl, as if to say, "Where's breakfast?"

Nicole pushed herself out of bed and staggered to the bathroom. When she came out, she looked into Cindy's room and discovered her sister was already up.

"She's as bad as the cats," Nicole muttered to herself.

Mollie was another story. "Time to get up," Nicole called, but the sprawled heap beneath the covers slipped farther down toward the foot of the bed.

"Come on, Mollie," Nicole commanded.

A tousled blond head poked out, its expression as cross as a bear's that had been disturbed too soon from its winter hibernation. "Have a heart, Nicole!" Mollie pleaded. "It's supposed to be vacation, remember."

"I know." Nicole sighed. *"Quel dommage!"*

"Can't we sleep in just once?" Mollie begged as her sister turned toward the door. "We don't have anything to cater today."

"But the big city council luncheon is tomorrow, and there's a lot to do." Nicole refused to relent. "Move!"

By the time Nicole had consumed several cups of coffee and half a grapefruit, Cindy had returned from her jog and Mollie had finally crawled out of bed. The three girls climbed into the station wagon and set off.

Nicole put Mollie to work slicing vegetables, gave Cindy some flour to sift, then sat down with several cookbooks to do some serious scrutiny.

"Is this luncheon tomorrow the last job we have to do?" Cindy removed her Walkman headphones to ask, her voice hopeful.

"Uh-huh." Nicole nodded absently.

"Thank goodness," Cindy said, trying not to

spill flour over the counter. "How many cups did you say, Nicole?"

"*Mon dieu.* Pay attention, Cindy!" Nicole snapped. "The recipe's right in front of you."

"Touchy, touchy," Cindy murmured. "We're almost through with this nightmarish job, Nicole. Can't you lighten up, for Pete's sake?"

"I'd like for at least *one* job to go perfectly," Nicole told them, her tone still aggrieved. "Just one—before we have to tell Mother about all the problems. I meant everything to go so well, and all we've had is one disaster after another!"

"It hasn't been that bad," Cindy protested.

"You call knocking out the guest of honor not bad!" Nicole threw up her arms. "Not to mention hanging coats on his prize sculpture."

"How was I to know?" Cindy grumbled. "It didn't look good for anything else."

Nicole threw her a dark look, then went back to her recipes. Her mother had planned a very impressive menu for the city council and their guests. Nicole would have to use all her culinary talents to pull this one off. But surely the sisters could get one job right—and Nicole wouldn't be left feeling like an utter failure. She had to pause several times to answer the phone and courteously turn down several more jobs for her mother's catering business.

When she had compiled the list of ingredients they needed for tomorrow's luncheon, Nicole handed the paper to Cindy, who had completed her sifting, and who—under a light dusting of flour—looked almost ready for baking herself.

"Here's the food to order, and the numbers of the suppliers. We need these items delivered quickly," she warned her sister. "So wipe the flour off your nose and get busy."

The sound of the bell from the front door alerted the girls to a visitor.

"I'll get it," Nicole said.

To her surprise, she recognized the tall young man at once.

"Rob! What are you doing here?"

Then Nicole, feeling that her impulsive greeting lacked tact, added, smiling, "I mean, I don't suppose you need a dinner catered?"

Rob grinned. "Not any time soon. I tried to phone, but your line has been busy all morning."

"We've had a lot of business calls," Nicole explained. She couldn't quite conceal the pleasure she felt at seeing him again.

"I have the afternoon off," Rob explained, his tone a bit tentative. "And there's a special showing of foreign films at the college. I thought you might like to go."

"I'd love to," Nicole told him, her voice heavy with regret. "But I've got work to do."

"You couldn't get away for just a couple of hours?" Rob suggested, looking so disappointed that Nicole felt even more tempted. "I may not have any more time off this week."

"I'd better not." Nicole shook her head. "I have

to keep an eye on my sisters, or who knows what might happen in the kitchen."

"I like that!" an indignant voice said behind them.

Nicole whirled. "Mollie! Are you eavesdropping again?"

Mollie ignored her sister's note of censure. "Cindy and I can handle everything for a while; we've got lots of time before the luncheon tomorrow. Don't treat us like idiots, Nicole. Go see the movie. I certainly would." She batted her large blue eyes at Rob.

Nicole fumed. The little brat! But perhaps Mollie was right. Nicole had been working herself to a frazzle for days. Surely Cindy and Mollie could manage by themselves for an hour or two.

"Can you give me ten minutes?"

"Sure." Rob's warm smile sent a shiver down Nicole's spine. "I'll be out in the car."

Nicole flew back into the kitchen.

"Who set your apron on fire?" Cindy asked as she dialed the next number on her list, the seafood supplier.

"I'm going out for a little while," Nicole said. "Cindy, you make sure we get all the supplies ordered and delivered by this afternoon. Mollie, I'll finish adding the ingredients for the sheet cakes, you mix them, pour them into the pans— *carefully*—and bake them. I'll decorate them when I get back."

Mollie nodded, wishing that she could slip away

from the shop, too. But she brightened when she remembered that tonight was the party at Alex's house—and from the address, she suspected that he lived in a real mansion. Talk about exciting! Mollie, suspecting shrewdly that Nicole would not be as thrilled, hadn't yet mentioned the date with her newest conquest. So despite the impulse to tell her sisters all, she shut her lips firmly and watched Nicole add ingredients to the huge mixing bowl.

"Now all you have to do is mix and bake. Okay?"

"I'm no dummy," Mollie retorted.

"Fine, I'll be back soon."

Nicole grabbed her purse and hurried out the door. Both girls watched her go, wishing they could walk out behind her.

"I'm so tired of cooking," Mollie mumbled to herself.

Cindy, her ear still glued to the telephone while she waited for someone to answer, said, "You think you have troubles; I'm stuck with this old crab who's as crusty as his crustacea!"

Her sudden expression of alarm revealed that her impatient words had been heard by the wrong person. "No, no, Mr. Antonio, I didn't mean—"

But the person on the other end didn't seem disposed to listen to her apology.

"I'm sorry, really," Cindy insisted, pale beneath her tan at the thought of having initiated another disaster.

Perhaps it had been a bad week for Mr. Antonio, too. Cindy winced at the torrent of invective that hurled itself through the phone line. "I am not a disrespectful, impertinent twit! I didn't mean—"

Finally the angry buzz from the other end of the line ignited Cindy's quick temper, and she sputtered into the phone. "Just because you're older doesn't mean you can yell at me and I can't yell back! Maybe you are the biggest crab in the warehouse, is that my fault?"

Her indignant shout made Mollie turn, alarmed. Cindy took the receiver from her ear and stared at it in disgust. "He hung up on me!"

"Oh, dear," Mollie gulped. "Which one was he?"

"The seafood man," Cindy told her. "And Nicole wants three-dozen pounds of lobster by tomorrow morning. What am I going to do?"

"Call back and apologize?"

"I tried." Cindy's frown deepened. "He wouldn't listen. There must be somewhere else I can buy some lobster."

Unfortunately for the girls, large quantities of lobster seemed to be in short supply in Santa Barbara. Cindy made half a dozen more calls to order all of Nicole's required ingredients, but the lobster meat was still missing.

"Please," she pleaded with the last man on her list. "Somebody must have some lobster meat to sell. No, I don't need any ground chuck. Wait." Cindy had a flash of inspiration. "I'll take the ground chuck if you can tell me someone who has some lobster . . . right."

Cindy scribbled a number on her pad and hung up.

"Did you find another supplier?" Mollie asked anxiously as she began to pour batter into a collection of sheet pans.

"Maybe," Cindy told her. "This guy says he's never done business with this firm, but he heard them mentioned at the warehouse." She dialed the new number, adding absently. "You have to grease and flour those pans before you put in the batter, Mollie."

"Oh, crumb." Mollie moaned. "I forgot." She poured the first panful of batter back into the big bowl and hurried off to get out the flour.

By the time the cakes were safely in the oven, Mollie saw Cindy pick up the car keys.

"Did you find the lobster?"

"Yes." Cindy grinned, her good spirits restored. "And at a fantastic price, too. Lots cheaper than Mom's regular supplier. I have to go pick it up myself, from a truck down at the dock, but that's no problem. I'll be back before Nicole returns—I hope! Don't say a word to her; you know how she'll fuss."

"I won't," Mollie promised, relieved that their problem had been solved. Hardly had Cindy walked out the door when the bell in the front signaled a caller. Mollie, attempting to smooth her hair as she glanced into the gleaming reflections on the refrigerator door, hurried to the front room.

No handsome young man awaited her, to her private disappointment, but it was a surprise almost as good.

"Sarah! Linda! How great to see you," she told her two friends from school.

"We called you at home, but no one answered," Linda said. "Then we remembered that you were helping out at the shop. How's your mom?"

"Doing great," Mollie told them. "What have you two been up to? I've really missed you."

"I know, seems like a month since we've seen you," Sarah said. "And my life is a disaster, Mollie."

"What happened?"

"Sarah broke up with Andrew," Linda explained.

"Oh no," Mollie exclaimed. "That's terrible. Tell me everything."

The ensuing tale, which involved several phone calls, one visiting cousin from San Diego, and several complicated misunderstandings, was naturally engrossing. Who could blame Mollie for forgetting her task in the kitchen?

Not until the sudden shrill ring of the telephone broke the spell of conversation did Mollie realize that more time had gone by than she'd intended.

Sarah sniffed. "Is something burning?"

"My cakes!" Mollie shrieked, running for the ovens. She grabbed heavy oven mitts and began to pull the blackened sheet cakes from the ovens.

Meanwhile, Sarah, unable to bear the insistent ringing, hurried to help her friend by lifting the receiver of the telephone.

"Hello, this is Movable Feasts Catering," she said courteously. "I'm sorry, Mollie can't come to the phone right now, but something's burning, and—" She stopped and stared at the receiver. "They hung up!"

All three girls stared glumly at the crusty, darkened cakes. "What can you do, Mollie?" Linda asked.

"Throw them out and start over, I guess." Mollie sighed.

"Can we help?"

Mollie considered but finally shook her head. "Better not. If we start talking again, I'm liable to add chili powder instead of cinnamon to the batter, and then where would we be?"

The two girls giggled and said good-bye. Mollie, wishing she'd never seen an oven in her life, began to scrape out the blackened mess.

In the college theater lobby, Nicole banged down the phone.

"What's the matter?" Rob asked, alarmed.

"I *knew* I shouldn't have left them alone," Nicole raged. "I'm sorry, Rob. I had a wonderful time, but I can't stay for the second film. I've got to get back to the shop before they burn the building down."

"In that case, we'd better hurry," Rob observed sensibly, and they rushed out to his car.

Cindy, pulling back into the parking space behind the catering shop, hurried to unlock the rear door and pull out the heavy cartons. One of the cardboard flaps was undone, and Cindy, for the first time, glanced inside at the packages of frozen seafood she had bought. Did they look a little squishy—as if they weren't, perhaps, completely frozen? No, that couldn't be. She had driven straight back from the dock, and the truck from which she'd received the large carton had probably been refrigerated, Cindy assured herself. No one would sell frozen food that wasn't properly handled. Now if only Nicole didn't find out—

She headed for the back door, only to walk straight into a heated battle.

"How could you ruin the whole batch of cakes?" Nicole yelled. "I was only gone an hour! And where's Cindy?"

"Right here," Cindy said. "Just putting these boxes into the freezer."

"I can't leave this place for an instant." Nicole fumed. "I thought you two had learned a little responsibility. Why do I have to be the only one with any sense—"

"Now hold on, Miss Priss." Cindy, her hands free at last, turned to face this unfair attack. "I've worked hard for over a week, I haven't been surfing once—"

"Talk about the ultimate sacrifice." Nicole sneered. "I could do a better job with one hand tied behind my back. You two have been nothing but a big liability."

"Listen, you creep!"

Mollie, miserably certain that it was all her fault, put her hands over her ears and missed the next few adjectives that flew furiously from one sister to the other.

Only when Cindy threw down a wooden spoon and stalked toward the door did Mollie take her hands away, just in time to hear Cindy yell, "Fine, Your Highness! If you think you can do a better job alone, I'll just get out of your way! This hasn't been exactly a fun-filled job, you know!"

When the door slammed behind her, Nicole stamped her foot. "Who needs you!"

Mollie, her blues eyes full of guilty tears, looked anxiously at her oldest sister. "Do you want me to leave, too?"

Chapter 11

"*It really was all my fault,*" Mollie said, sniffing. "I'm sorry, Nicole."

Nicole, whose anger seldom lasted long, found her righteous indignation fading rapidly beneath her little sister's teary gaze.

"It's all right, Molly. You don't have to leave. Let's get these cakes baked one more time."

"What about Cindy?"

"She'll get over it. And she'll feel better after an afternoon at the beach."

Nicole began to pull out the big sacks of flour. With her there to supervise, this time the baking proceeded smoothly, and within a few hours they had a whole row of sheet cakes cooling on the counter.

"Can I help decorate?" Mollie asked, pleased

that they were coming to the interesting part of the baking.

"Better let me," her older sister answered. "This is tricky, Mollie, and I really want everything just right tomorrow. It's our last job for Mother, and I'd like to go out with a flourish." Nicole, intent on proving her abilities as an adult in a job that had seemed so simple in the beginning, didn't notice Mollie's disappointed look. "You can polish the silver trays that we'll use to serve tomorrow."

Mollie sighed. Another grungy job—as usual. How disgusting that Nicole still thought of her as a baby! Then Mollie remembered her approaching evening with Alex. Going out with a sophisticated older man—Mollie wasn't sure how old Alex was, but he certainly was a complete hunk—should make Nicole realize that she was underestimating her little sister. Content with the knowledge that there was some justice in the world, Mollie went to the pantry to take out the silver polish.

When the two girls finished for the day, leaving the cakes carefully covered in the big freezer and everything else ready for Nicole to finish Tuesday morning, they drove home in weary silence.

Nicole, glad to be almost finished with their unexpectedly arduous assignment, found the house empty except for the animals, all of whom rushed eagerly to see her.

"Down, Winston," she commanded automatically. "I'll feed you in a minute. Hi, Smokey." She paused to pet the cat, looking for signs of Cindy. Her stubborn sister would still be at the beach, of course. Nicole felt a small tremor of guilt, remembering the harsh words she had hurled at her, then pushed the feelings away. Cindy would get over it. And the middle Lewis had definitely committed more than her share of foul-ups this last week!

There was a note from their dad on the bulletin board; he would be home a little late. Nicole fed the animals, then headed for the stairs. A quick nap before she started dinner sounded heavenly. She sank down on her bed and was asleep almost before her head touched the pillow.

Mollie took a quick shower and dried her long blond hair carefully, coaxing it into smooth waves that made her—she hoped—look older than her fourteen-and-a-half years. She spent extra time on her makeup, glad that Nicole had disappeared into her room and couldn't lecture her on overdoing it. Then came a hurried search through her closet to find an outfit that would be most sophisticated. As usual, nothing looked appealing. The tangerine jumper that had looked so great in the boutique suddenly seemed not quite right. Maybe with a lime-green belt?

Mollie fussed with her clothes for an hour, wishing that she could borrow a few items from Nicole's closet. How did her older sister always manage to look so perfect? Life was so unfair.

But at last, after Mollie had tried on most of her current favorites and had come full circle to the tangerine jumper she started with, with a lemon turtleneck underneath, she picked up her highest heels and tiptoed down the stairs.

In the kitchen, Winston woofed at her.

"Shut up, Winnie," Mollie hissed. "I know perfectly well you've already been fed, so forget it. And I don't want Nicole waking up just yet." She scribbled a note on a sheet of paper, stuck it to the bulletin board that served as the Lewis family message center, and, grabbing a sweater, hurried out the door. She was glad that Alex had told her to come early for dinner. Not only was it still light outside, but she wouldn't have to answer her dad's questions.

Not until she was on the bus did Mollie breathe easier. Now for some real adventure!

She rode silently, lost in a glorious daydream where she dazzled all of Alex's sophisticated friends with her understated elegance and charm. Several good-looking young men elbowed each other to compete for her attentions, while Alex fumed in the background. Then the bus drew up to her stop, abruptly ending her fantasy.

"Oh." Mollie waved at the driver and scrambled to get off. Almost stumbling on her high heels, she jumped down from the last step and looked eagerly around her as the bus drew away with a last puff of smoke.

"What a neighborhood!" Mollie looked up and

down the wide street, impressed despite herself. The Lewis home was certainly not small, and Mollie loved its comfortable, attractive furnishings, but the houses that lined this street were large enough to awe any normal teenager. Set well back behind carefully tended lawns, with long driveways winding through artfully scattered trees and shrubs, these houses were truly something out of the ordinary.

Mollie walked along the wide avenue until she located the right street number, turned toward the entrance, and came face-to-face with a large locked gate.

"Oh, dear," Mollie murmured. "Now what?" She inspected the impressive brick posts and wrought-iron gate, finally noticing a speaker. For a moment she hesitated, then remembered she *had* been invited. She pushed the button.

After a breathless moment, an accented voice said, *"Sí?"*

"Mollie Lewis, for Alex's party." Mollie tried to make her tone confident and was rewarded when a buzzer sounded and the large gate swung open automatically.

She breathed easier and began to make her way down the curved drive. But Mollie's heart still pounded, and despite her earlier daydream, she began to hope that there wouldn't be too many guests.

"Just a small party," Alex had told her. "A few friends dropping by." How many were a few? Not *too* many, Mollie hoped. They would all be strangers, and perhaps they wouldn't be impressed with Alex's new discovery as she had wished. And, oh no, what if her clothes weren't right?

On this dreadful note, Mollie approached the big house. It was an impressive mock-Tudor, with lots of arches and exposed beams. Through an arched drive, she counted only five cars parked in the back courtyard, so perhaps there wouldn't be a horde of people present. Encouraged, Mollie walked up the front steps and rang the doorbell.

Another alarming thought almost paralyzed her vocal cords. Would Alex have a butler, some awesome figure with an English accent?

But when the big door swung open, Mollie saw a plump woman in a dark uniform who didn't look awesome at all.

"Sí?" she inquired.

"Buenos días," Mollie stammered, remembering belatedly that it was too late in the day to say good morning. Oh, well, it was the thought that counted. "I'm here to see Alex."

"Entre," the servant told her. "Alex—in back."

Waving vaguely toward the hall, the woman disappeared through a doorway, leaving Mollie on her own.

Good grief. Now what? A house like this should come with a map that said, "You are *here*." Mollie peered uncertainly through the nearest doorway. She saw a large, elaborately furnished drawing room, with a rug that was surely genuine Persian, and which Mollie would have died before stepping on. She backed away quickly and tried another room.

This was a dining room, with a table that looked big enough to seat half the freshman class at Vista High. Mollie, awed by the sight of all that gleaming wood, shook her head.

Feeling more and more as if she had accidentally strayed into an episode of *Masterpiece Theater,* Mollie tried another doorway.

This room appeared to be a library; shelves of leatherbound books stretched all the way to the high ceiling. Mollie, who enjoyed an occasional good story, stared at the collection with wide eyes. An air of unreality clung to these shelves filled with matched sets of books with gilt-edged bindings, as if she had stepped into a stage setting rather than a real room for real people. She dared to slip one heavy volume from its place on the shelf and flipped it open.

The pages weren't even separated; how could anyone read a book like this? Mollie wrinkled her brow as she pondered this question, when a voice from behind made her start.

"I thought I heard the bell. Are you into Socrates?"

Mollie turned quickly, a guilty flush on her cheeks. "I didn't mean—I'm sorry, Alex."

"No sweat," the young man told her cheerfully as Mollie eased the book quickly back onto the shelf. "These books were ordered by the decorator, anyhow. The paperbacks my mom really reads are upstairs in her bedroom, and my dad only reads the *Wall Street Journal.* Glad you could make it, Mollie. Come meet the gang. Did you find a place to park your car?"

Mollie, gulping, couldn't think of an answer, but fortunately Alex didn't seem to notice. He led the way through the house while Mollie tried to keep track of their path. They came at last to a wide room with lots of plush couches and glass tables, and an assortment of strange-looking sculptures that reminded Mollie of the art gallery where she had met Alex for the second time.

"Are your parents interested in modern art?" Mollie asked, pleased that she had managed to get her brain working again.

"Oh, Dad thinks of art as an investment, and Mom buys what the decorator tells her to." Alex grinned. "Hey, everyone, this is Mollie."

Heads turned at the casual introduction, and Mollie tried to keep up with the names that were flung her way. A tall brunette in a silver lamé outfit that won Mollie's complete admiration waved a languid hand; another girl in a low-cut knit top and khaki pants tried to turn a yawn into a semipolite greeting. The young men present eyed her with more enthusiasm. A lanky redhead came closer to shake her hand, pressing it with such unnecessary firmness that Mollie quickly pulled it from his grasp. And a short, plump boy with shaggy hair winked at her, adding, "Hey, Alex, where do you find all these attractive young women?"

Alex grinned, and Mollie, a trifle pink but flattered, too, followed him to the bar at the end of the room.

"What would you like?"

Alex waved casually at a collection of bottles that made Mollie's eyes widen.

"Uh, lemonade would be fine."

Alex threw back his head and laughed. "Mollie, you're such an original! With a dash of grenadine?"

"Plain is fine," Mollie assured him nervously.

"Whatever you say, doll."

He handed her a tall, frosty glass, and Mollie followed him back to one of the couches, sipping cautiously at the pale liquid, relieved to find the fruit juice untainted. She sat down beside the plump boy, who to her alarm immediately slipped closer. She tried hard to think of something sophisticated to say.

"Where do you go to school?" she asked finally, unable to think of any other conversational opening.

"Oakwood."

"Is that a college?" Mollie asked, trying to gauge the boy's age.

He grinned. "No, a prep school. Very high-class, you know? I'm just home for spring break."

"Can't be too high-class if they let *you* in," the girl in the silver lamé outfit pointed out, and the whole group laughed.

"I'm at Saint Cat's," Sachi, the dark-haired girl, volunteered. "And you?"

Wondering if all of Alex's friends went to private schools, Mollie said hastily, "Uh, I'm on spring break, too."

"She gave up a cruise to help her mother out," Alex told them. "Her mom had to have surgery, and Mollie and her sisters have taken over her catering business for the time being."

"Your mother caters? How quaint," Sachi murmured, managing to make the innocuous remark sound like an insult.

Mollie bristled. "She's the best cook in Santa Barbara, and we're proud of it," she declared angrily.

"Hey, I think that's cool," the stout boy assured Mollie. "I'm into liberated women!"

Mollie couldn't think of a reply, so she sipped her lemonade and tried to smile in a liberated fashion.

"I'm taking a cruise to the Norwegian fjords this summer," the red-headed boy told them. "My mom thinks it'll be educational."

"If there are any Scandinavian beauties on board, you'll manage to make it educational, all right." The stout boy smirked. "Did I tell you about the Swedish girl I met in London last year?"

"In nauseating detail, Todd." Sachi looked bored. "Don't start with the adolescent chest-beating again, spare us, please!"

While the group laughed, Mollie stared at her lemonade, feeling distinctly out of place.

"Where were you going on your cruise?" the other girl asked in a deceptively sweet tone. "Have you been through the Panama Canal yet?"

Mollie, wishing she hadn't been quite so expansive, tried to think how to explain that she had only planned a weekend trip to Catalina.

Fortunately they were all distracted by the entrance of the maid, carrying a large tray of dishes.

"I think dinner is served, guys," Alex told them. "How about some linguine?"

Mollie, glad for the diversion, joined the rush toward the table and tried to enjoy the elaborate spread of food. But, in fact, the food wasn't half as good as her mother would have prepared, and Mollie was beginning to feel that Alex's friends spoke a different language. She certainly wasn't enjoying her evening as much as she'd anticipated.

Perhaps some of her discomfort was reflected in her expression, because Alex came back to her side and said quietly, "What's the matter, doll? Don't you like my friends?"

"Of course," Mollie assured him quickly, not knowing how to explain her discomfort. How could Alex understand? He seemed like a nice guy, but Mollie was beginning to feel that they came from different sides of the world—maybe even different planets!

"We're not very lively tonight, I know," Alex

told her. "But they're not a dull bunch most of the time."

"Oh, I'm not bored," Mollie assured him.

"Well, I am." Sachi, overhearing this last remark, came closer to lean on Alex's arm, her manner deliberately possessive. "Why don't we try out the hot tub, Alex. Maybe then the party will really get going."

"Why not?" Alex agreed. "Anyone for the spa?"

A chorus of assents drowned Mollie's involuntary gasp, and the rest of the group headed toward the patio, obviously familiar with Alex's home.

"Aren't you coming, Mollie?" Alex flashed his lazy grin, and Mollie wavered, not sure she wanted to compete with the voluptuous Sachi in a borrowed bathing suit. If only she had her new mauve bikini!

"I didn't bring my bathing suit," she explained.

"You're such a riot." Alex grinned. "Who needs a bathing suit? Come on, the spa's out back."

Mollie, gulping hard, wasn't sure that she'd understood. "Are you serious?"

Alex's bland expression convinced her more quickly than any protest.

"I mean, uh, in a minute. I need—where's the powder room?"

"Oh." Alex nodded. "Just off the front hall. Come on back when you're ready."

"Sure," Mollie agreed, and scurried off to find the bathroom.

Safely inside the lavatory, Mollie stared into a

large gilt-framed mirror at her own reflection.
Nude?

For about five seconds, Mollie considered the
idea. Then, overcome by a furious blush, she
shook her head. Alex's crowd probably thought
nothing of it; some people went to nude beaches
all the time. But not Mollie Lewis.

She considered leaving Alex a note telling him
she might be ready for his parties in about twenty
years but then decided to skip it. She tiptoed
back toward the front door and let herself out
very quietly. Then she hurried down the front
drive, relieved to find that the gate was not locked
from the inside, and found herself back on the
wide avenue. She walked very rapidly down the
side of the street, a little nervous at being alone
in the cool dark night.

She thought about what would happen if her
parents ever found out about the hot tub, or if
Nicole ever found out about the party. Then, looking up to see a city bus approaching the corner,
Mollie broke into a run.

Chapter 12

*C*indy *rose early Tuesday morning and dressed* in comfortable sweats for her usual jog. When she returned to the house, feeling comfortably spent, she headed for the shower, surprised to find that Nicole and Mollie had already left.

"Of course," she murmured to herself. "The big city council luncheon is today. Nicole must be having fits."

For a moment she felt an unpleasant sensation of loneliness, as if she'd been left out of a family party. Not that this will be any party, she told herself ruefully. Not with Nicole cracking the whip!

So who cared, anyhow? It was great to be free to go to the beach and meet all her friends. Whistling briskly to show just how contented she was, Cindy came out of the shower and dressed in her favorite faded blue swimsuit, with ragged cutoffs and a T-shirt thrown over it. Skipping down the stairs, she consumed a large bowl of cereal. When Winston nosed her hopefully, she shook her head. "I can't take you today, Winnie." She strapped her surfboard to her bike, threw a towel around her neck, and headed for the beach.

She found Duffy and Anna already assembled at their favorite spot. "Hi, you double-crosser," Cindy yelled at Duffy as he splashed throught the water, while Anna stretched out on the sand. Dropping her towel, Cindy hastily stripped off her shorts and T-shirt and headed for the ocean.

Despite the chill of the water, which made her gasp when she took her first plunge, it was a beautiful day. Blue skies and high clouds, bright sunshine and a slight breeze had lured dozens to the ocean. A storm off Baja California had done its part by sending hearty waves to the Santa Barbara beaches. The sunlight glittered off the water while the waves rolled in, crashing against the sand with rhythmic force. All in all, it was a day to delight a dedicated surfer.

Cindy lost no time in pursuing the perfect wave, yet the feeling of nagging discontent was hard to ignore. In a few minutes she made out a familiar form, and she waved happily at Grant, who soon paddled out on his own board. Together they flew across the water, propelled by the powerful waves, laughing when Cindy took an unexpected spill.

After an hour, Cindy pulled her board back up to the beach.

"Tired already?" Anna asked.

Cindy shook her head. It was a perfect day, but she just couldn't enjoy it. She thought of the last time Mollie had come to the beach and her one abortive attempt at surfing. Tossed by a hard wave, she'd almost lost the ridiculous bikini she'd insisted on wearing. Mollie, torn between the practicality demanded of surfers and the allure of high fashion, made her decision quickly. Adjusting her very becoming bathing suit, she had spent the rest of the day lying on the sand. Cindy grinned at the memory, then her expression altered quickly to a frown.

Why couldn't she get her sisters off her mind?

Anna, content to lie with her head on an inflated cushion improving an already perfect tan, looked puzzled. "What's the matter, Cindy? Aren't you happy to be released from K.P.? Is your mother back home?"

"Not yet," Cindy said. "And I didn't get released, exactly. I walked out."

"How come?"

"Nicole was doing her drill-sergeant routine again just because I made a few lousy mistakes. If you could have heard what she said to me!"

"And what did you say?" Anna, who had known Cindy for years, grinned.

"Never mind." Cindy snorted. "Okay, so I did

deliver a few choice remarks myself. But she deserved it."

"Are you going back?"

"Not till Nicole apologizes." Cindy shook her head. "If she thinks she's better off without me, so be it."

"You're not usually a quitter," Anna murmured.

Cindy gritted her teeth; she had enough people mad at her already. Swallowing her quick retort, she pretended not to hear her friend's remark. "What'd you bring to eat?" she demanded, looking into her friend's big tote bag. "It was great of you to volunteer to make lunch today."

"I thought you'd be tired of cooking." Anna grinned. "Hey, those ham sandwiches are supposed to be for lunch. It's only ten o'clock."

"But I'm starved."

"You're always starved," Anna pointed out.

Cindy shrugged and reached for a soft drink to go with the sandwich. She pulled out a can, wrapped in layers of newpaper to keep the liquid cool.

"Why don't you get another cooler?" Cindy asked.

"I meant to, but I spent all my allowance on my new bikini." Anna glanced down at her scarlet-and-black outfit with a complacent smile.

"Honestly," Cindy said, shaking her head. "You're becoming as bad as Mollie."

"Anyhow, you ought to make a contribution,"

Anna said. "If you hadn't stepped on the old cooler, it wouldn't have cracked."

"If Grant hadn't hit the volleyball so far from the net, I wouldn't have fallen over the cooler," Cindy explained. "I'll pitch in, though, as soon as I get some money."

"I won't hold my breath." Anna grinned.

Cindy took a bite of her sandwich, while her eyes fell on the scrap of newspaper. "Dozens ill from tainted seafood," the headline read.

Cindy sat up straighter, and the tender ham in her mouth began to taste like sand.

It couldn't be!

She grabbed the paper and read on. "Dozens of Santa Barbara restaurantgoers report serious outbreaks of food poisoning. Lobster meat supplied by J. D. Smith wholesalers is suspected. Public health officials are following up the reports ..."

Cindy groaned.

"What's wrong with my sandwich?" Anna asked. "You look positively green."

"How many seafood suppliers named Smith do you think there are in Santa Barbara?"

"What?"

"Never mind." Cindy dropped the barely eaten sandwich and jumped to her feet, grabbing her clothes and hopping madly around as she struggled to pull them on. "Ask Grant to take my surfboard home; I haven't any time to wait for him. I have to get to the shop."

"What's wrong?"

"I've got to stop a poisoning!"

Anna stared after her in shocked astonishment, but Cindy didn't notice.

Inside the catering shop, Nicole looked over her handiwork with a sigh of pleasure. Her hours of hard work had produced satisfying results. The canapés were packed and ready to transport; the salad greens fresh and crisp, ready to toss; the cakes, frosted and decorated, ready to go. Last but certainly not least, the lobster thermidor, her *pièce de résistance,* was packed carefully into coolers. The savory meat, removed from the lobster tails, diced, cooked with cream and mushrooms and other seasonings, then returned to the shells and dusted with Parmesan cheese, looked truly irresistible.

Surely this last assignment would go perfectly, and when Nicole finally told her mother the whole story, she'd have at least one unblemished job to report. Then Nicole could stop feeling like such a failure! She and Mollie had worked hard all morning. She hated to admit it, even to herself, but Nicole had definitely missed another pair of hands. Drat Cindy for deserting the ship, anyhow! Nicole knew Cindy's temper well, but she'd thought surely the middle Lewis would have gotten over her snit and returned to the shop by now.

"Mollie, hurry and bring out the last box," Nicole called now. "I don't need another traitor in the ranks."

Mollie, taking a well-deserved break with a tattered paperback, sniffed. "That's not fair, Nicole," the youngest Lewis protested. "I've toiled like a galley slave all morning."

"Are you reading that same novel again?" Nicole asked.

Mollie bristled. "Historical novels are educational. Mom said so."

"I don't think you're reading for the history." Nicole sounded skeptical. "Anyhow, bring out the last package. I need *someone* to help me."

Mollie complied with her sister's order. "It's not all her fault, Nicole. You did yell at Cindy."

"Well, she yelled at me," Nicole pointed out. "Help me get this last load into the station wagon; I've got to get across town and set up for the luncheon. This is our last job, and our most important; it's just got to go well."

"Relax," Mollie urged, as she followed Nicole to the station wagon. "Your food will be great. Good grief, where am I going to fit?"

"I don't think you will," Nicole admitted, examining the station wagon with a critical eye. Even the front seat was full. "You'll have to take a bus over while I deliver all the food and linen, then you can help me set up the tables and pass the canapés."

Mollie looked sulky, but after an irate glance from her older sister, she exclaimed, "Okay, okay."

"Don't fool around and miss the next bus," Nicole warned, turning the key in the ignition, when an unexpected arrival made them both look up in surprise.

Cindy, out of breath from her long ride, threw her bike on the ground and waved frantically at Nicole.

"You can't take the lobster, Nicole. It's no good," she called.

"*Mon dieu,* Cindy," Nicole snapped. "You insulted my food enough yesterday, don't start again."

"No," Cindy yelled. "Wait, it's no good!"

But her words were drowned out by the screech of tires as Nicole pulled angrily away from the shop.

The two younger Lewis sisters watched her go.

"That wasn't very smart, Cindy," Mollie observed, shaking her head. "After the fight yesterday, you shouldn't make comments about her recipes. Nicole has worked—"

"I'm not talking about her recipes." Cindy sounded ready to scream. "It's the lobster, you dummy. It's not any good."

She thrust the scrap of paper before her younger sister. Mollie read the article twice, once in astonishment, and again with an expression of horror on her face. She appeared ready to burst into tears.

"What are we going to do?"

"I don't know, but we have to stop Nicole from serving that lobster. We can't let the whole city council be poisoned!"

"Would they die?" Mollie gasped.

"I don't know, they might." Cindy, despite her interest in biology, wasn't at all sure just how serious food poisoning could be. "But Mom might never be able to cater again. Her business would be ruined!"

"Oh, Cindy." Mollie gasped. "It's all our fault. Do you think they'll put us in jail?"

Even Cindy, the eternal optimist, blanched. "I doubt it," she stammered, her voice full of uncertainty.

Mollie, whose vivid imagination conjured up visions of suffering patients all pointing accusing fingers, like the Ghost of Christmas Future, at the Lewis sisters, choked back a sob.

"It's all my fault." Cindy groaned. "If I hadn't argued with Mom's regular supplier, this never would have happened."

"How could you know the lobster was spoiled?" Mollie tried to allay her sister's guilt, but her own expression was still worried. "We've got to let Nicole know."

"We can't explain all this on the telephone, especially if she won't listen to me to start with. We'll take the bus over to City Hall. But, Mollie, then what?"

"What do you mean?"

"What about the luncheon Mom promised them? All those people are expecting to be fed."

"We'll have to cancel it, I guess," Mollie suggested.

"Mother's never had to cancel a job, and with

the city council, too! That would ruin her reputation just as thoroughly as serving tainted food. We have to come up with something else to feed them, Mollie."

Mollie looked alarmed. "Without Nicole? *We* don't know how to cook anything!"

"But there isn't time to bring Nicole back." Cindy paused, momentarily nonplused. "What are we going to do?"

Mollie brightened. "When Mom and I were driving back and forth to L.A. for my auditions, when I thought I might get a part on a new sitcom, you made tacos one night, remember? They weren't bad, Cindy."

"You think so?" Cindy looked hopeful again. "There's all that ground chunk in the freezer, and we've got plenty of fresh vegetables. And I made chili for a team cookout once. The guys even came back for seconds."

"The polo team will eat anything," Mollie pointed out, but Cindy refused to be discouraged.

"Nobody got sick!"

"Well, that's something," Mollie agreed. "But what will we say to Nicole—replacing her elegant recipes with tacos and chili?"

Cindy frowned, then a glimmer of inspiration appeared in her mind. "I have an idea —you remember that shawl and embroidered skirt Mom brought back from her last trip to Mexico?"

While she explained, both girls went to work. Cindy threw the ground chuck into the large microwave to thaw and began to mix the ingredients for the chili, while Mollie grated cheese and chopped vegetables for the tacos and heated refried beans.

"What about taco shells?"

"We'll have to stop at the market and buy some."

"How are we going to get all this to the luncheon?" Mollie suddenly asked. "Nicole has the station wagon. We can't take all this food on the bus!"

"We'll have to; I don't have enough money for a taxi." Cindy, despite an alarming vision of overloaded arms, sounded determined. She measured spices into the chili, crossing her fingers and throwing in one extra spoonful of chili powder just for luck.

It was probably the fastest meal that had ever been thrown together in the big kitchen. They were assembling the last of the food when the sound of the bell alerted them to a caller.

"Maybe Nicole forgot something," Cindy said hopefully, then shook her head. "She wouldn't come to the front door. I'll get rid of whoever it is."

She hurried into the front room and stopped in surprise at the sight of a familiar face.

"Grant! This is great!"

"I knew you'd be delighted to see me, but I didn't think you'd be overwhelmed." He grinned.

"You left the beach in such a hurry, I thought I'd better check to see if you're all right."

"I'm in a real jam, but you can help," Cindy told him. "It's not you I'm so glad to see, it's your car!"

Grant chuckled. "Talk about putting me in my place."

"Come help us load the food," Cindy said. "I'll explain on the way."

Chapter 13

*N*icole wrinkled her brow, gazing around the crowded room at the assembled dignitaries. She had the champagne flowing, and the guests obviously appreciated the canapés, but the buffet table was still not completely set out. She couldn't do *everything* by herself! Where on earth was Mollie?

Probably still immersed in her book. Nicole fumed. She should have stuffed her little sister into the trunk with the linen.

A handsome older woman with short gray hair almost covered by an elegant cream-colored hat stopped in front of Nicole.

"Nicole Lewis? How you are, dear?"

"Mrs. Carlton," Nicole faltered, recognizing one

of the more vocal members of the city council. "How nice to see you again."

"We met when your mother catered my cousin's daughter's wedding," the older woman explained.

What a memory this woman has! Nicole thought fleetingly, then focused her attention hurriedly back on the woman's words.

"When I heard that Laura Lewis was catering this luncheon, I knew that the food would be superb," the woman continued. "Where is your mother, dear?"

"Uh," Nicole stammered, her usual poise momentarily deserting her, "she had emergency surgery last week, so she's been ordered to stay away from the shop for a while."

"My goodness. I hope she's recovering rapidly."

"Yes, thank you. My sisters and I are helping out today." Nicole glanced around wildly, as if Mollie might pop up on cue, and hoped the councilwoman wouldn't ask about the rest of the Lewis clan.

"I'm sure you've had excellent training, dear. The city council luncheon is in capable hands. A good thing, too, as we have some important guests today."

Nicole, hoping that the comment hadn't been meant to intimidate, felt her knees turn to jelly.

"Yes, ma'm," she agreed weakly. Where was Mollie?

"Allow me to introduce one of our special

guests," Mrs. Carlton continued. She motioned to the men beside her. "This is Mr. Shin and Mr. Akito, who are studying our city for possible industrial development."

The two Japanese businessmen greeted Nicole in excellent English, bowing as they spoke.

Nicole quickly bowed back, trying to look suitably poised, but her inner turmoil increased. It was almost time for the luncheon to begin. How could she get all the food out by herself? Where was Mollie? If anything happens to ruin this meal, I'll never be able to face Mother, Nicole thought. She was so certain that this one last job was going to be perfect.

Mrs. Carlton glanced at her diamond-studded watch. "I believe it's time to take our seats for the preluncheon introductions, gentlemen. And we don't wish to keep Nicole from her duties."

Recognizing a hint when she stumbled over one, Nicole smiled weakly and hurried back to the buffet table. The salad was ready, and the cakes, adorned with miniature American and Japanese flags, looked splendid. But the lobster thermidor had to be removed from the cooler and placed on the table before the guests could help themselves. Under cover of the introductions, Nicole hastened to the back room, where the rest of the food waited.

Pausing in the small room behind the council chambers, Nicole blinked. The cooler containing her main course was missing!

"Mon dieu!" Nicole strangled a scream with the back of her hand. "The lobster's been kidnapped!"

She thought she might faint. Who could have done this? The back door led onto an alley; Nicole rushed to push open the unlatched door and peer down the alleyway. If she nourished wild hopes of discovering a mild-mannered derelict loaded down with a huge cooler of lobster thermidor, she was doomed to disappointment. The alleyway was empty, and her entrée still missing.

"C'est terrible!" Nicole moaned. "What am I going to do?" She leaned against the wall, holding her aching head in both hands. From the room beyond, she could hear the loudspeaker boom as the introductions were at last completed.

"I believe we're ready now to help ourselves," the anonymous voice queried. "Is that correct?"

Nicole groaned. Instant disgrace—how would her mother ever live this down? Nicole would have to go into the room and announce to a whole roomful of VIPs that their lunch had been abducted!

But the voice continued. "Ah, I see our pretty hostess is ready. What? Oh, we have an announcement."

Mon dieu. What on earth was going on? Nicole pulled herself together and hurried through the doorway, where she could see the front of the room.

To her bewilderment, a quick glance at the buffet table revealed their mother's largest soup tureen, steam rising from its contents while Cindy quickly set out large trays of—could it be tacos?

"Mon dieu," Nicole repeated hopelessly. The whole world had turned upside down. Cindy had decided to discredit her sister forever. "Cindy, how could you?" Nicole gasped.

Then she turned back to see Mollie step up to the microphone, wearing an outrageous costume of brightly embroidered skirt, peasant blouse, and gaily colored shawl, with a large Spanish comb in her blond hair.

"It's a conspiracy," Nicole murmured. "They're *all* out to get me."

"Buenos días, señores y señoras," Mollie cooed into the mike. "We welcome you to a genuine southwestern-style luncheon. *Bon appétit!*"

Nicole groaned again at this hodgepodge of languages, waiting for the whole room to rise up in righteous protest.

But although a couple of the city council members looked a bit startled at this abrupt change in menu, the visiting Japanese smiled broadly at Mollie's innocent enthusiasm, and their American hosts, quickly taking their cue from the visitors, relaxed and bowed them on to the buffet table.

Nicole, trying to breathe normally, managed to make her way to the long table, where she hissed at her middle sister.

"Cindy, what's this all about?"

Cindy, observing Nicole's purple face, pulled her older sister aside.

"The lobster meat was spoiled," she whispered. "There've been cases of food poisoning all over the city. We had to think of a quick replacement; it was the best we could do, Nicole."

Nicole reeled from the thought of their near disaster. Both sisters had forgotten their recent quarrel; only the threat to their mother's business seemed important now.

"Thank heavens you discovered it in time," Nicole exclaimed.

Cindy, guiltily aware that she would have to explain later just how it was that they had ended up with tainted seafood, merely nodded.

"Is the chili edible? I mean," Nicole amended quickly, watching the guests sample the potent mixture with expressions of surprise but not, to her relief, distaste, "I'm sure it's fine, Cindy. And I'm proud of you both for such quick thinking."

Cindy beamed at this unusual praise. "I'm sorry I ran out on you, Nicole. You know I wanted to help Mom as much as anyone."

"It was my fault, too," Nicole told her ruefully. "At least now I know who kidnapped the lobster!"

Cindy grinned. "It's in the station wagon. I thought of throwing it into the harbor for the gulls, but I was afraid we might poison them!"

Mollie, pushing futilely at the large comb, which kept threatening to slide off her head, appeared beside them. "Everyone seems to like our food. What's so funny?"

But the other two, hysterical at the thought of

threatening the iron-stomached seagulls, were momentarily unable to explain, and they collapsed against each other, overcome with laughter and relief.

Chapter 14

*W*hen everything had been cleared away and Mollie had discarded her impromptu costume, the girls took the dishes and trays back to the shop, cleaned and put away all the utensils, and finally made their way home.

"I've got to call Grant and thank him again," Cindy was saying as they pulled into the garage. To their surprise, their father's sedan sat on the other side.

"You don't think something's wrong with Mom?" Mollie said, worried.

"Of course not," Nicole said, trying to feel as confident as her words. "Dad's just home early."

But they all hurried into the house nonetheless. Richard Lewis sat at the kitchen table, drinking a cup of coffee.

"Hi, Dad. What's up?" Cindy demanded.

Their father looked at them thoughtfully.

"How were things in the shop today?" His tone was bland, but Nicole felt a stab of fear.

He knows something! She and the other two sisters exchanged quick, guilty glances.

"Uh, fine," Nicole stammered. "Why do you ask?"

Richard Lewis stirred his coffee and said only, "Don't worry about starting dinner, Nicole. We'll send out for a pizza later. Your mother wants us to come straight to the hospital."

Nicole paled. "Nothing's wrong with Mother?"

"No, no, she's fine." To their chagrin, Mr. Lewis would say nothing more. They all climbed into his big sedan and made the short journey in silence, with the three girls trying not to look as guilty and concerned as they felt.

When they reached their mother's hospital room, they were surprised to see her sitting on the edge of the bed, fully dressed.

"Mom, where's your gown?" Mollie asked.

"The doctor said I can go home. He's even allowing me to look into the catering shop next week, if I stay off my feet and leave the heavy work to others."

"That's great, Mom," Cindy exclaimed. "What a terrific surprise!"

"Yes," Laura Lewis agreed. "I wanted to leave the hospital days ago, but the doctors were determined to be extra careful. However, I received another surprise today."

The three girls, alerted by her change in tone, exchanged glances once more. Their mother held up a slim envelope. "Your dad brought me the mail from home this morning, and guess what I found in the middle of the circulars!"

Nicole groaned. She had been so careful to screen the mail, but she'd finally missed something.

"A letter from Carol," their mother went on. "Postmarked from France! She apologizes again for leaving me without any warning and hopes everything is fine at the shop."

There was a dreadful silence, and Nicole felt her face flush. Looking around, she saw that embarrassment was epidemic; all three Lewis sisters had red faces. Cindy chewed on her lip, and Mollie looked about to cry.

"It's my fault," Nicole said quickly. "I accept the responsibility. We just wanted to keep you from worrying about the shop."

"I agreed," Cindy said stoutly. "It's just as much my fault."

Mollie added, "Mine, too."

"We didn't mean to deceive you," Nicole tried to explain. "We didn't know when we decided to help at the shop that Carol had already quit so that she could marry Jim and go to Europe with him. But when we found out, we were afraid to tell you. We didn't want you trying to come back to the shop too soon."

"We were worried about you," Mollie put in.

Their mother seemed puzzled. "But, girls, what about all our catering engagements this last week and a half? Did you cancel them?"

"Oh, no," Cindy exclaimed. "That was the whole idea; we took care of everything."

Laura Lewis looked somewhat taken aback. "You catered a whole wedding—by yourselves?"

They all nodded. "Nicole did a beautiful job on the cake—except for the feathers, but I got them off, and if we hadn't hit the chicken truck, that would never have happened," Cindy explained in a rush.

"And I met a gorgeous guy," Mollie confided, "though really not my type. And you should see the hunk Nicole found at the art gallery; he didn't even get mad when Cindy hung coats on the prize sculpture."

Laura Lewis shut her eyes for an instant, and Nicole threw an angry glance at her sisters.

"We really did pretty well, Mother, *c'est vrai.* We haven't had any complaints, not any *serious* ones, anyhow. I—I really wanted our catering to be perfect, but I guess I'm just not as capable as I thought I was."

At Nicole's dismal confession, Mrs. Lewis opened her eyes quickly. "Nicole! Professional catering is much more complicated than it appears; I'm sure that you did a marvelous job, especially at such short notice! If you knew half the mistakes I made during my first few years of catering!"

Nicole's woebegone expression lightened slightly. *"Vraiment?"* If her superefficient mother could make mistakes, then Nicole needn't feel like such a failure.

"I think we have three terrific cooks here, to have handled the shop on their own." Their father grinned. "Or should I say tough cookies?"

"Please!" Nicole groaned.

"Do you girls remember the time your mother tried to make a Saint Patrick's day meal and ended up with green hamburgers?" their dad asked. "No one would eat them, not even Cindy, and Winston had hamburger meat for a week!"

They all laughed together, and Cindy looked thoughtful. "I do remember that. And what about the giant cake for the supermarket opening?"

"The one that fell into a hundred pieces from its own weight?" Their dad finished the story.

Mrs. Lewis threw up her hands. "Don't remind me of all my disasters!"

Richard Lewis smiled tenderly at his wife. "That wasn't a disaster. You used the crumbled cake to make a sherry trifle that was completely delicious, and considerably enlivened the ribbon cutting. Talk about snatching victory from the jaws of defeat!"

They laughed again. "We've had a few of those kinds of victories ourselves," Nicole told her parents. "Wait till we tell you about our genuine southwestern-style luncheon."

"I can't wait," Laura Lewis said. "But first let's

get out of here! And while I start interviewing for a new assistant, you three can have a few days' well-deserved vacation before school starts again."

"Great," Cindy said as they all collected armloads of flowers to take out to the car. "But no chili for the next month, please. I think tasting our genuine southwestern-style chili all morning burned a hole in my stomach, not to mention my tongue!"

Here's a look at what awaits you in OUT OF THE WOODS, the tenth book in Fawcett's "Sisters" series for GIRLS ONLY.

Nicole and Cindy retreated to their own tent and stared at the precarious balance of their sister, her sleeping bag, and the none-too-secure V-shaped hammock. They had a feeling they wouldn't have to stare at it too long.

On the other side of the campfire, Mollie was suffering. Her legs were entwined with each other more than she thought they ought to be, but they were also scrunched up next to her body and surrounded by her arms. She was lying on her right arm and even after just a few minutes, it was clear her arm would be the first part of her to sleep, followed immediately by her left ankle. Why did her ankle hurt? Well, Mollie couldn't even begin to figure it out, but, as far as she was concerned, pain was pain and she was in it. That thought made her scratches start throbbing. Maybe they were becoming infected. Suddenly, not only did everything hurt, everything itched, too, and there was just no way she could maneuver to scratch any part of her body. Maybe she had fallen right into a patch of poison ivy and tomorrow she'd be covered with ugly red splotches.

She listened carefully. She could hear her sisters talking, but there were other sounds, too. The leaves on the ground nearby rustled. Probably just a squirrel, Mollie thought. It got louder. Winston growled. Must be a raccoon. Winston barked. Winston *always* barked at raccoons.

But Winston also barked at bears.

Mollie tried to picture what was going on outside by the sounds near the campfire, by the direction of Winston's barking, and by the loud rustling around. She heard some branches snap underfoot. It would take something very big to snap so many twigs with a single footstep. And that something very big was coming very close to her.

Next, she heard the animal prowling around her tent. She could hear the pages of a magazine rip. Winston continued to bark and growl. It sounded like things were being thrown around inside her tent—just the way they had been before. Then the sounds stopped. There was silence for a few seconds.

The rustling began again and came closer and closer to her hammock. Something tugged at one of her saplings. Her hammock bounced on the ground. Mollie realized that the creature, whatever it was—and by now, she was absolutely certain it was a bear—was tugging not at the tree, but at her failed bedside table. She realized that it was made of aluminum—nice shiny aluminum, just like the cans of soda, which she'd placed in the stream, that had attracted the bear.

Then, for the first time, it occurred to Mollie that she could scream. She could scream her head off and her older sisters would come running to her rescue. They would frighten the bear off with whatever it took—shouting and screaming, or wrestling the beast to death. Mollie decided to scream. But she couldn't. No matter how hard she tried, she couldn't get a single sound to come out of her constricted throat. She was simply too terrified.

The beast stopped tugging at her night table and began tugging at one of her saplings.

Bears can't climb saplings, she reminded herself. No bear in his right mind would climb a tree that couldn't hold his weight.

Then she realized it didn't matter if bears could climb saplings or not. No bear would have to climb a sapling to attack her. She was only six inches above the ground. That was probably exactly the height of a bear's dining table, Mollie thought, miserably.

Finally, there was a tremendous jerk at one of the trees. It brought to an end the perilous balance of Mollie's hammock. The entire construction collapsed. Mollie, instead of being in a hammock that might dump her at any time, now found herself in a sack in which she was a helpless prisoner.

She found her voice at last. *"Help!"* she cried. "Cindy, Nicole, help me! The bear is attacking me! I'm stuck here. Come help me before I'm ripped to shreds! *HELP!*"

There was no answer to her cries. At first, Mollie thought her sisters must have fled, but then she realized that they never would have had a chance against the bear. It occurred to her that the bear might have eaten them first. But then why would he still be hungry?

Ugh! What a thought! But where were Cindy and Nicole? Mollie screamed again, hoping she could make enough noise to draw someone from another campsite before the fatal attack.

Finally, she heard human noises, and relief rushed through her. She was sure her rescuers, whoever they were, could chase the bear away before it ate her. She waited for the melee to begin.

It didn't.

Instead, she realized through the haze of vanishing

terror, the noise she was hearing was laughter—uncontrolled, smirking, snorting, giggling, human laughter.

"Get me out of here!" she demanded.

"As soon as we can, Mollie," Cindy's voice assured her.

"Why can't you do it *now*?" Mollie asked.

"Because we're laughing too hard," came a familiar male voice.

It was Paul Markham.